WINNING DR. WENTWORTH

BOOK TWO

REBECCA HEFLIN

WINNING DR. WENTWORTH

Published in the United States of America by:

Rebecca Heflin Books, LLC

www.RebeccaHeflin.com

ISBN: 9781736660065

❋ Formatted with Vellum

ACKNOWLEDGMENTS

As always, I must thank my beta readers, Yvonne, and my hubby Ron. Thank you for your continued guidance, patience, and support.

For my introduction into the world of sports analytics, I'd like to thank Will Pantages with the University of Florida. His discussion on how collegiate sports teams collect and utilize statistics was invaluable. I did, however, take some creative license, so any inaccuracies are purely my own.

And to my editor, Paul, thank you once again for catching and correcting my errors. I couldn't publish my stories without your keen eye.

"Boys love football, girls love football players,
and some girls love football and football players."

– Unknown

1

M urphy's Law ruled her life.

Shelby Wentworth tossed her backpack across the console onto the passenger seat of her car then dropped into the driver's seat and slammed the door shut. Closing her eyes, she took a deep, cleansing breath. At least, she *tried* to take a deep breath. After the contentious conversation with her ex-husband, the pain in her chest made it difficult to breathe.

Would she ever be able to leave the past behind and focus on rebuilding her career? Her life?

Pressing a hand to her sternum, she counted to five as she inhaled, held her breath for another five-count, then exhaled. The breathing exercise slowed her racing heart and calmed her. "That's better," she murmured.

Starting the car, she threw it into reverse and backed out of her spot in Sterling University's faculty parking lot.

And right into a solid object.

The sickening *crunch* set her heart racing at warp speed this time.

Glancing behind her in horror, all she saw was a big gray behemoth.

With trembling hands, she put the car in park and jumped out to find a late-model dark gray Suburban, it's rear passenger-side fender crumpled, but little damage otherwise. Her old Honda Civic, on the other hand, hadn't stood a chance against the tank she'd backed into. The trunk was crumpled, and her bumper hung off the passenger side in a lopsided grimace.

Out of the corner of her eye, she saw a tall, athletic man stride around the back of the SUV.

Fear swamped her, and she covered her mouth with both hands. "Oh my god, I'm so sorry! Are you okay?" Bracing herself for the tirade, she backed away from him, holding her hands out in front of her.

"No harm done."

What? That's it. No yelling? No name-calling? No threats?

He adjusted his red Sterling Bobcats ball cap, leaning down to assess the situation then scratched his chin and stood up. "Okay. Maybe a little harm done," he said with an easy smile. "Question is, are you okay?" He removed the aviator sunglasses he wore and directed his concerned gaze right at her.

"Nash?" The instant she saw those electric blue eyes, she recognized him. Butterflies took flight in her stomach, and not from fear this time.

He'd been powerfully built in high school, but that had been just a preview to the powerfully built man he would become. And although he'd left the NFL, he hadn't lost his quarterback build. The son of former NFL quarterback, Carl Taylor, Nash had been destined for greatness.

They hadn't seen each other since the day they'd graduated high school. But, despite her broken heart, she'd secretly followed both his college and pro football careers.

She'd been watching the day of the NFL draft, five years earlier, when the Denver Broncos called his name and he'd gone down on one knee and proposed to his college sweetheart, Stephanie Cummings, further adding to her heartbreak.

She'd also been watching the Broncos versus the Raiders the day he'd taken the hit that had ended his career.

And finally, she'd witnessed the press conference when Nash Taylor stood, tears in his eyes, as he gave up the sport he loved at the young age of twenty-seven, his beauty-queen wife noticeably absent.

It wasn't long after that news of their divorce hit the headlines.

"Shelby?" he asked, his surprise evident in his expression.

"You remember me?" she couldn't help asking.

"Of course." He frowned. "Why wouldn't I remember you? We were best friends back in the day."

Were being the operative term.

A flush crept up her neck and into her face as she recalled her first kiss in the backseat of their best friend's car. But the flush turned to heartache at the memory of Nash's later betrayal.

"I thought your mom moved. Are you here visiting the university?" he asked.

"No. I, uh, I took an assistant professor position in the College of Arts and Sciences." A step down for her, but she'd been lucky to get even *that*. She toed a piece of her car's bumper that had fallen off in the collision.

"No kidding?" He rocked back on his heels. "How long have you been back?"

"I moved two weeks ago. I'm surprised I haven't seen you before now." She knew he'd moved back to his hometown of Sterling after he'd left the NFL and became the head coach of the newly formed Bobcats football team. It was the one of the reasons she'd hesitated in taking a job she'd so desperately needed. Being in the same town—and a small one at that—as Nash would be a constant reminder that she'd never really gotten over her high school crush.

"I've been . . . out of town." He shoved his hands into the front pockets of his jeans.

"Oh." She nodded as if she understood, but really she didn't. Clearly there was more to that statement. An awkward silence fell.

"Look, I know the new police chief. Let me give him a call so we'll have a report for the insurance companies." He pulled a smartphone from his back pocket.

"Oh, but—" She'd really rather just pay for the damage than deal with the insurance . . . and have them raise her already-too-high rate. "Can we just handle it between ourselves? Of course I'll pay for the repairs."

"You sure about that?" He paused in tapping out the number.

"Yeah." A nervous laugh escaped. She'd just add it to the long list of bills she currently struggled to pay. Maybe Nash would take it in installments for old times' sake. "Why deal with all that paperwork?"

"I can't let you do that."

～

Shelby wrapped her arms around herself, the body language unmistakable. She nodded. "I'll get my insurance information." She turned back to her car.

"No. I mean I can't let you pay out of pocket. And don't worry about the insurance. The deductible is probably more than what it would cost to repair the damage." He could think of a better way for her to repay him. "How about you buy me dinner instead and we'll call it even?"

She looked good, Nash thought. Better than good. The pretty tomboy had grown into a beautiful woman. She'd cut the long, light brown hair that as a teenager she'd worn almost exclusively in a ponytail, so that it just touched her shoulders, and she'd filled out in all the right places.

The shy smile was still there, although he didn't miss the sadness in her amber eyes. Or the fear when he'd first approached her.

"What?" Confusion skittered across her face.

No surprise there, considering he was just as confused by his offer as she was.

He grinned. "You know, the meal you have at the end of the day? In the South we call it supper, in case you've forgotten."

She'd lost some of that innocence he'd found so appealing so many years ago. Along with her accent. Guess that's what happened when you received an Ivy League education.

She looked away and then back at him. Her eyes narrowed. "I just nailed the back end of your car, and you want me to have dinner with you?"

He had an all-consuming urge to gather her in and hold her close until the tension in her shoulders, and the sadness and fear in her eyes, retreated. But he doubted she would accept his sympathy. After they'd both left for college, he'd tried to hold onto their friendship despite the distance, but she never answered his emails or phone calls.

He knew he'd hurt her in high school when he took Leandra Lucas to prom instead of her, but he'd made a promise to a friend, and he didn't break promises.

"Yeah, why not? Catch up. It's been, what, eleven years since I saw you?" The day they'd graduated in fact. Him with decent grades and a football scholarship, and her as class Valedictorian. She'd headed off to Brown University for an accelerated program in mathematics the following week, and he hadn't laid eyes on her since. Not even for their ten-year reunion last year.

She bit her lower lip then drew it into her mouth, and his eyes locked on like a heat-seeking missile. The memory of the sweet, hot kiss they'd shared in the back seat of Ethan's 1993 Ford Mustang assaulted him.

"I don't think that's a good idea."

She was probably right. He just nodded. Clearly, she hadn't forgiven him for what he'd done. Not that he could really blame her. He should have been upfront with her then. She would have understood. Maybe.

"I should probably give you my number so you can get me the repair bills for your car if you change your mind," she said, returning his attention to the present.

"Right." She stepped close and a light, clean scent tickled his nose. Like lemons, only sweeter. He tapped the number into his phone as she rattled it off to him, all the while wondering whether she wore perfume or if it was her shampoo. "But I won't. Change my mind, I mean."

"Okay. Well. Again, I'm really sorry about . . ." Her voice trailed off as she indicated the fender-bender.

"It's just a car. Nobody got hurt, and that's the important thing."

"I'll see you around." Shelby rounded her car and climbed into the open driver's side.

Realizing she couldn't leave until he moved his car, he turned to do just that, but couldn't help but wonder what twist of fate had brought Shelby Wentworth back into his life.

SHELBY PULLED up in front of her apartment building and exited her damaged vehicle, slinging her backpack on her shoulder as she walked to the front door.

Her wrecked car would have to stay that way for now. Glancing back at it, she contemplated the lopsided bumper. First, she had to ensure that Nash's would be repaired, despite his assurances to the contrary. And come up with the money to pay for it.

After years of being publicly berated for her mistakes, Shelby had expected the same from the guy whose car she'd just smashed. Once she'd recognized Nash, though, she knew better. His calm, cool demeanor in the face of a defensive blitz was one of the reasons he had been an NFL first-round draft pick.

The polar opposite of the man she'd spent the last five years with.

Of course she'd run into Nash at some point. After all, with a population around sixteen thousand—and that included the university students—Sterling was no Atlanta. She just didn't expect to *literally* run into him.

She stopped by the mailbox, dreading what she'd see—

more bills she couldn't pay. Thumbing through the pile, she almost considered putting them back in the box.

What a day! A hot bath, a glass of cheap wine, and a juicy romance novel were at the top of her Friday night to-do list. And since Sterling didn't offer much in the way of nightlife—unless you were a twenty-something college student—it was a safe bet she wouldn't be missing much.

Nestled in the hills of northeast Georgia, the town of Sterling owed its existence to two things: granite and knowledge. Granite because it held some of the richest granite quarries in the world. If it was made of granite, it probably came from Sterling. And knowledge because Sterling University, one of the Southern Ivy League schools, educated almost ten thousand students each year inside its hallowed halls, and sent them out into the world to share that knowledge.

Established in 1835 by wealthy granite quarry magnate and town founder Samuel Sterling, the university's arts department even offered classes in granite carving. And of course its geology program was one of the country's best. Sterling had endowed the university with one million dollars and three hundred fifty acres of land adjacent to the family home.

When the last of the Sterling line, Victoria Eliza Sterling-Pickard, died in 1974, she left the family home to the university for use as its main administration building, aptly named Sterling Hall.

If you lived in or around Sterling, you most likely either worked for the university or for one of the many surrounding granite quarries or monument makers.

Which meant everyone knew everyone else's business.

Just as she stuck her key in the lock, her neighbor's door opened.

"Oh, hi, Shelby!"

Delaney Driscoll had been her first new acquaintance since coming back to town, not that they'd done anything other than exchange pleasantries at the mailbox, but Delaney was warm and friendly.

"Hi, Delaney. Heading out for the evening?"

"Yeah, I'm meeting a friend." She locked her door then looked up. "Hey! Why don't you join us? I mean, I know you already know people in town, but Sam's really terrific. I think you'd have a lot in common since you're both big-time researchers."

Big-time researchers? Well, maybe Delaney's friend was, anyway. She glanced longingly at the door that led to peace and solitude. And another evening filled with self-recriminations and figuring out how to pay the bills she currently held in her hand. "I don't know. I wouldn't want to impose . . ." Not to mention spend money.

"It's no imposition. Come on. It'll be fun."

Teetering on the edge of saying no, she reversed course. Why not? Maybe some girl time would do her good. She'd been holed up in her apartment since moving in. Not because she was busy unpacking—she'd left with little more than a few personal belongings, just what would fit in her car—but because going out meant potentially running into former high-school classmates that still called Sterling home.

Which meant questions about what she'd been doing and why she was back. Questions she wasn't up to answering yet, if ever.

"Okay. But should I change?" She glanced over at Delaney's bombshell figure, flatteringly displayed in a red silk blouse, black skinny jeans, and sky-high stilettos, then looked down at her own blue jeans, rust-colored blouse, and serviceable ballet flats.

"Nah." She waved her hand. "You look great." She shrugged, "We're just going to McGinty's Pub. Burger and beer night."

"Let me drop off my stuff and I'll be right out."

"Sure. Hey, what happened to your car?" Delaney asked.

"Don't ask."

2

Forty-five minutes later, Nash walked into the locker room at Granite Fitness, wiping sweat off his face with a towel, and came face-to-face with his best friend, Ethan Quinn.

As the new dean of the College of Arts and Sciences, Ethan already had his plate full, but he always managed to squeeze in a workout.

"You done?" Ethan asked as he threw a towel around his neck, his sweat-free appearance a clear indication he hadn't worked out yet.

"Yeah. You just getting started?"

"Yep. Sam and I had an appointment with the florist."

"The florist? Damn, she's got you wrapped." Ethan and his fiancée, Dr. Samantha Love, were tying the knot next spring, and wedding plans had just begun.

"Yeah, she does. And I wouldn't have it any other way," he said with a grin and a wink.

Nash had never seen Ethan so happy. And why shouldn't he be? He had the deanship he'd worked so hard for, he had a smart, beautiful woman in his bed every night, and his latest book was due out next month. The man was living under a lucky star.

"Hey, did you know Shelby's back?" Ethan asked as he bent over to tie his shoe.

"Yeah, I just ran into her. Or, should I say, she ran into me? Literally."

At Ethan's puzzled look, Nash told him about the fender-bender with Shelby.

"She okay?"

"She's fine." Oh, so fine. But hurt—at least emotionally. "Hey, what about me? I'm the innocent bystander here," he said, tongue firmly tucked in his cheek.

Ethan snorted as he stuffed a pair of jeans into his gym bag and stuck it in a locker. "You took hits from three-hundred-pound defensive linemen for a living. I think you can withstand a tap on the bumper of that tank you drive."

Nash pulled his sweaty T-shirt over his head, and began drying off with the towel, recalling Shelby's fear. "What do you know about the reason for Shelby's return?"

Shrugging, Ethan said, "Only that her ex-husband and former mentor had falsified research data. There was a big investigation resulting in journal retractions, his termination from Stanford University, and prohibition from any future research involving federal dollars."

"Damn." No wonder Shelby was gun shy. "And Shelby?"

"She was innocent but decided a change of scenery would be best, so she resigned from Stanford and took an assistant professor position here—a demotion for her. But, it's going to take some time to shake off the taint of her ex-husband's betrayal."

"She's essentially starting over," Ethan continued as he

rose. "She has no articles or papers to her credit, except her dissertation. A death knell to anyone seeking tenure." Ethan filled his water bottle from a dispenser. "It would be like you trying to get into the NFL draft without your college stats."

Why did life have to kick the shit out of people like Shelby? Good people. People who worked hard, told the truth, and trusted their fellow man?

Like she'd trusted him, only to have that trust betrayed. He winced. "Why did you hire her then?"

"She deserved a fresh start."

Yeah, that was Ethan. Although it probably didn't hurt Shelby's chances that she and Ethan had been best friends back in the day too. The three of them had been as thick as thieves growing up.

"Sam's going to dinner with Delaney tonight," Ethan interrupted his musings. "Got any plans?"

"Nope." Especially since Shelby turned him down. "What do you have in mind?" Toeing off his athletic shoes, he dug around in his gym bag for a bottle of shampoo.

"Burger and beer at McGinty's?" Ethan offered.

"Sounds good. I'll wait for you, and we can walk over together. I've got some new plays I can review while I wait."

"Works for me. I won't be long. Just going for a quick run on the treadmill," Ethan said as he headed out to the gym. Stopping before he reached the door, he asked, "What about tomorrow?"

"Nothing, other than taking my car over to Mac's Body Shop in Carlyle for an estimate." With the Labor Day weekend, he'd given the team the day off after practicing hard all week. He wanted them fresh and ready for next week's home-opener against Cornell.

"Sam and Delaney are driving into Atlanta to go dress

shopping, so it only seems fitting that I take my best man to Atlanta to look at tuxes."

Nash held back his groan. After all, how many times would his best friend get hitched? He pointed at Ethan, "In that case, you're buying tonight."

"Deal."

"Oh. No. He. Didn't!" Samantha said, her eyes wide with shock.

"Oh. Yes. He. Did!" Delaney replied, a look of disgust on her face. She'd just regaled them with the details of her latest blind-date-gone-wrong—with the new middle school principal from Sterling's exclusive all-boys private school. Delaney crossed her fingers over her heart, "God's truth."

"What did you do?" Sam asked as she scooped the olive from her martini.

"I told him, in no uncertain terms, that I did not want to go back to his place to see his . . ." she shuddered, "iguana."

Sam snorted. "Is that what they're calling it these days?"

Shelby couldn't stop giggling. She really needed this. More than she'd realized. Sipping on an ice-cold Cosmo, nibbling on fried pickles and cheesy nachos, and dishing with two smart, funny women.

She wouldn't think about the hit to her wallet from the cocktails, appetizers, and entree she'd ordered. Just add it to the rest of her debt.

She really liked Sam. A psychology professor in the same college as Shelby and Delaney, she'd recently hit the news with her latest discovery the press called "the love test" —a blood test that determined compatibility. One of the largest online dating services in the U.S. now offered it as part of their premium package.

Sam was everything Shelby wasn't. Polished, confident, beautiful.

But the best thing about Sam and Delaney—they didn't know anything about her Great Career Suicide or GCS for short, so she had nothing to prove to them. They had no preconceived notions about Sterling High School's Valedictorian, voted Most Likely to Succeed.

And she'd missed female camaraderie. When she and Charlie had been married, they'd rarely socialized, and when they did it was usually with another group of researchers, most of whom were men. Charlie didn't approve of girls' nights out. Or alcohol. Or fun, for that matter.

It was true that you can't judge a book by its cover. Charlie had a nice cover, but once you flipped through the pages, he was nothing but a poorly written villain.

Delaney flagged down the waitress and ordered another round before happy hour ended. Shelby could already feel the delightful effects of one Cosmo. She polished off her drink and licked her lips. At this rate, they'd need to take a cab home. Wait. Did Sterling even have cabs now? Or Uber? Not that she could afford either one. Last resort, she could always walk the five blocks to her apartment.

"Okay. Enough of that." Delaney drained the last of her margarita. "It's time to talk wedding." She rubbed her hands together with glee. "What have we got?"

The bride-to-be lifted several thick bridal magazines from the bench seat next to her and set them on the table. Colorful tabs fanned out from the pages marking things that interested her.

She turned to the first tabbed page and spun the magazine to face Shelby and Delaney. They both released collective sighs. Shelby hadn't had a traditional wedding. She and Charlie married at City Hall because Charlie thought weddings were a waste of time and money. She'd never thought of herself as a bride—couldn't even remember what she wore.

Suddenly she wished for the opportunity to wear something so beautiful when she married the man she loved.

Which was utterly preposterous since she'd never place her heart, her trust, and especially not her career, in the hands of a man again.

"Do you like it?" Sam asked, her well-manicured hands folded beneath her chin, a hopeful expression on her face.

"What's not to like?" Delaney asked as she ran her fingers over the glossy photo and read the description. "'A floor-length ecru silk ottoman dress, bateau neck, with lush overskirt.' It's so . . . you."

Although Shelby and Sam had just met, she completely agreed with Delaney. The gown was simple, elegant, and tasteful.

"And I can remove the chapel-length overskirt for the reception." She pointed to the photo on the facing page of the simple sheath dress beneath the overskirt.

"It's perfect." Delaney's eyes looked suspiciously moist.

"Hello, ladies."

Gasping, Sam slammed the magazine shut and hugged it to her chest.

Shelby looked up into Ethan Quinn's smiling brown eyes. Even more handsome with eleven years added. He'd thrown her a lifeline when he approved hiring her in his college. Behind him stood Nash, looking every bit the former NFL quarterback in his worn jeans and Bobcats sweatshirt. Living in Small Town, USA, she knew she was bound to run into him, but twice in one day?

To SAY Nash was surprised to see Shelby at McGinty's Pub with Delaney and Sam would be an understatement. And, as people often liked to remind him, he was the master of understatement.

Shelby looked adorable with a lopsided smile, giving away her slightly inebriated state.

"Tell me you *did not* just see my wedding dress," Sam whispered to Ethan.

Ethan's eyebrows shot up. "You've already picked one out?"

"Yes, but if you saw it, it's a no-go."

He leaned down, stared into her eyes, and said, "Sweetheart, I didn't see a thing. Cross my heart."

Sam sighed as her eyes glazed over like she'd had her bell rung by a defensive lineman.

Nash shook his head at the two lovebirds. But also felt an unwelcome longing. His ex-wife had put his heart on injured reserve, but maybe it was time to get back in the game. His gaze found Shelby again.

"You boys want to sit down?" Delaney asked as she pulled Shelby toward her in the booth, leaving space for Nash to sit next to Shelby.

"Sure." Ethan slid in next to his bride-to-be, and they shared a tender kiss. "But only for a minute. We have man things to discuss," Ethan said, indicating Nash.

Man things? What the hell were *man things*?

With nothing else to do but join the group, Nash sat down, bumping his thigh against Shelby's. They shot a glance at each other at the contact, and her face registered her surprise at the sudden heat.

Yeah, they still had it. Question was, did she still want it? Because he'd discovered maybe he did.

"What kind of man things?" Delaney prodded.

"Oh, you know," Ethan shrugged, "Saturday night's match-up between Georgia and UNC, whether the Braves are going to get into the World Series, and world peace."

"Given Georgia's new five-star QB, I'd say they'll beat the Tarheels. Six-five, two-fifteen, one hundred twenty-five career TD's, six hundred fifty-nine completions, and total passing yards just shy of ten thousand . . ." Shelby shook her head. "He's a force to be reckoned with. And with the Braves' pitching staff ERA of three-thirty-five, sixty-nine wins, six hundred one strikeouts, and ten shut-outs, they should easily route the teams in the remainder of the regular season. As for world peace, well, statistics aren't in your favor there," Shelby finished with a sigh, her chin propped in her hands.

Nash sat speechless, Delaney's mouth hung open, and Sam's eyes widened.

"Damn, Shelby, you're still keeping up with Georgia sports?" Ethan asked.

Shelby shrugged. "I like sports, and I like statistics. Sue me." She popped a fried pickle into her mouth.

"You're a walking sports statistics encyclopedia." Ethan chuckled, picked up Sam's glass and took a gulp before swallowing and making a face. "Gah! How do you *drink* that?"

"What's wrong with a dirty martini?" Sam shot back.

"You mean, other than the dirty and the martini?" He signaled their waitress and ordered a whiskey on the rocks. Nash ordered a cold beer and stretched out his legs, settling in for what would clearly be longer than a minute.

"So, you and Delaney are off to Atlanta tomorrow to hunt for dresses?" Ethan asked as he helped himself to some nachos.

"Yes," Sam replied, another dreamy look on her face.

"Good. Nash and I are headed to Atlanta to look at tuxes. We can meet up for dinner before heading back."

"We can?" Nash asked, surprised.

"Sure, why not? There's a new eclectic restaurant in Buckhead I'd like to check out."

"Hey, Shelby," Delaney said, nudging her none-too-gently, "Why don't you join us?"

Shelby's brow furrowed, "Oh, no. I wouldn't want to intrude."

"You wouldn't be intruding, would she, Sam?"

"Of course not. The more opinions the better."

"It's settled then," Ethan said. "We'll meet you ladies at New Leaf at seven. That give you enough time?"

"Perfect," Delaney responded for them.

The waitress returned, her tray filled with drinks. Nash lifted a brow when she handed Shelby what looked to be another Cosmo.

Shelby raised the glass to her mouth and took a healthy pull.

"You're not driving tonight, right?" Nash leaned over and asked. Big mistake. Her warmth and scent enveloped him, turning his thoughts to driving her straight back to his place. Now.

Giving himself a mental shake, he realized it had been far too long since he'd been with a woman.

"No." She pointed to Delaney.

He looked across Shelby to see Delaney suck down a good third of her Margarita. "You're not driving tonight either, right?" he directed at Delaney.

"Not if I'm not safe. Uber." She popped a fried pickle slice into her mouth and broke into a stupid grin.

Definitely not safe, Nash thought.

He sighed, guess his boys' night out was turning into Nash's Taxi Service. No more alcohol for him, as it appeared he'd just become the designated driver.

3

Just as they all dug into their dinner, a voice from the past made Shelby cringe.

"Well, well, well. If it isn't Miss Most Likely to Succeed. Or should I say Mrs. Ingram?" Tonya Jordan raised her hand to her mouth in a fake show of chagrin. "Oh, that's right. You're divorced now, aren't you? Tsk, tsk. Such a shame."

Nash's body stiffened, and Shelby felt the heat of embarrassment in her cheeks. News travels fast in a small town. The glint in Tonya's eye reminded her why she'd been hiding out in her apartment since she moved back.

"Hi, Tonya," Shelby murmured.

"And that would be *Dr. Wentworth*," Ethan interjected, correcting both Shelby's title and her last name.

Tonya rolled her eyes. "A doctor? Is that what it's called when you play with numbers all day?"

"Don't be bringing that nonsense around here. We've got plenty of our own." Delaney wagged her finger at Tonya.

Tonya snorted.

"How's married life treating you, Tonya? Still playing the

trophy wife?" Nash wore a pleasant grin that didn't reach his eyes.

"Well!" Tonya gasped. "I never!"

"And you never will either," Ethan said, giving her a pointed look.

Tonya turned on her heel and left.

"Wow, what a beyotch," muttered Delaney.

Nash and Ethan had had her back since fourth grade. And apparently still did. The thought assuaged some of the humiliation, but Nash's rescue also confused her. Why would he leave her hanging senior year but stand up for her now?

"She's got no business throwing stones," Nash muttered as he plucked a fry off his plate and popped it into his mouth.

Shelby snorted. "She's the daughter of one of the richest men in town. Of course she can throw stones."

Ethan reached for the ketchup. "You've missed a lot in your eleven-year absence. Tonya's and her mother's lives took a turn for the worse when Mr. Jordan died."

Before Shelby could ask why, Ethan continued. "Turns out Mr. Jordan was in hock up to his eyebrows from keeping Mrs. Jordan and his daughter in the lifestyle to which they'd become accustomed."

"Not to mention a gambling problem," Nash added.

"The family sold the quarry," Delaney supplied. "And Tonya married the new owner out of desperation. A man twenty-five years her senior."

"Mr. Helsinger is closer to her mother's age than her own." Sam wiped her mouth with her napkin. "And is much tighter with the purse strings than Tonya's father."

"Karma's a bitch," Nash said.

"She sure is," Ethan echoed with a grin.

NASH POLISHED off the last of his fries and cast a glance at Shelby. The color had returned to her face. When she'd looked up and saw Tonya standing there, it was like watching a balloon deflate. Shelby had collapsed into herself.

Some people just didn't know how to be nice, not that Tonya would know "nice" if it came up and bit her on her now-fat ass.

As the conversation around the table turned to wedding talk, Nash recalled the day he first saw Shelby—the first day of fourth grade. He and Ethan had been engaged in a little friendly competition on the monkey bars when Nash noticed that Tonya and her four-feet-tall henchgirls had Shelby backed up against the chain link fence that enclosed the school playground.

Shelby had been the new kid in school, painfully shy, and rail thin.

One thing Nash and Ethan agreed on—bullies would not be tolerated, regardless of their gender or socioeconomic status. And Tonya Jordan was a bully.

He'd brought the situation to Ethan's attention and the two headed over to intervene.

Turned out Tonya was making fun of Shelby because, unbeknownst to her, she had been wearing one of Tonya's hand-me-down dresses.

He and Ethan had made it clear that day that Shelby was off limits and if either one of them saw Tonya or any of her mean girls so much as frown at Shelby, they'd tell Dirk "The Jerk" Michaels about her crush.

And to ensure nothing else happened after school, they'd walked Shelby home.

Even as Shelby put on weight and grew stronger from her physical activities, she learned to stand up for herself so that the bullies and mean girls were no longer a threat. Oh, they still teased her, but she no longer needed him or Ethan to stand up for her. She stood up for herself. But even then, unbeknownst to Shelby, he and Ethan had reinforced her own defenses with a few well-placed warnings of their own.

Despite her self-reliance, Nash had always felt protective of Shelby. And apparently still did.

From her reaction this afternoon and now, she'd lost her self-confidence somewhere along the way. Seeing her so cowed just made him mad. Mad at her dick of an ex-husband for taking that away from her, because he had no doubt he was at the bottom of this.

Ethan kicked Nash under the table. "You okay?"

"Yeah." With the warmth of Shelby's legs pressed up against his, her arm brushing his, her scent tickling his nose, he was more than okay.

THE WAITRESS DROPPED off the check and began clearing away the dishes.

Delaney picked up the folder, removed the bill, and looked at it, rubbing her temple with her free hand. "Oh, man! I can't figure this out. Why didn't we get separate checks?"

"Parties of four or more always get one check at McGinty's," Nash reminded her.

Talk turned to next week's football game, and Shelby watched as Delaney attempted to divvy up the bill. Her lips moved as she ran her finger over the receipt, apparently doing math in her head.

Shelby could've made short work of it, but she was reluctant to offer. She didn't know Sam and Delaney that well, and she didn't dare put herself out there like that yet.

But no one else at the table seemed aware of Delaney's struggle.

Nash finally leaned over, "Got it figured out yet, Einstein?" he asked with a wink.

"I think . . ." Her shoulders dropped. "No, I don't." She sighed.

"I'll figure it out." Taking pity on her, Shelby held out her hand for the bill. She took it from Delaney, quickly scanned it, then told everyone their portion, along with a twenty percent tip.

"Damn, Shelby. You're still a walking calculator too," Ethan said as he pulled some bills out of his wallet and slipped them into the folder.

"How did you *do* that?" Delaney asked in awe. Not waiting for a response, she rummaged around in her purse.

"It's easy." Shelby shrugged, handing Nash some money to cover her drinks, her portion of the appetizers, and the hamburger. This had been an unplanned—and irresponsible—splurge. Looked like a week of ramen noodles and cereal was in her future.

"No." Delaney began placing things on the table as she pulled them from a handbag the size of Shelby's overnight bag. None of which was her wallet. "It's not easy." Smartphone. Sunglasses. Hairbrush. Gum. "Math is not easy." Pack of Kleenex. Several lipsticks. Energy bar. "It's an unsolvable mystery, one that I abandoned after barely passing college algebra." Tampons. Condoms.

Nash chuckled and shook his head. "Interesting combo you got there."

Delaney ignored him and continued to fish around in what seemed like a bottomless pit.

Shelby reached over, her face hot with embarrassment, and pulled Delaney's wallet from the now-empty bag, then stuffed the offending items back in. "You just need the right teacher. I could show you sometime."

Delaney grimaced then swept the remainder of the items off the table and into her purse. "Thanks, but no thanks. I'd rather play with words."

"Come, woman. Let us away," Ethan said, taking Sam's hand and pulling her along behind him. She turned and called to Delaney and Shelby, "See you at eight in the morning."

Nash rose, followed by Shelby. Food had soaked up that second Cosmo and her encounter with Tonya had sobered her up. Unfortunately.

Delaney, however, struggled from the booth then stood, swaying on her feet.

"You okay?" Shelby asked.

"Yep. Never better." She missed her first attempt to scoop her purse from the bench. Then missed her second. Taking pity on her, Shelby grabbed it for her.

Nash chuckled. "You sloshed?"

"Lil bit," Delaney said, then giggled.

"All right." Nash stepped in. "Ladies, your chariot awaits."

"A chariot? I've always wanted to ride in a chariot," Delaney said with a slur.

"Now's your chance." He put his arm around her waist and directed her out the door, leaving Shelby to follow.

Guess Shelby knew who Nash was going home with tonight. Not that she could blame him. Delaney's blond hair, sexy curves and outgoing personality would make her appealing to any red-blooded male. Just like Leandra Lucas.

The burger she ate sat in her stomach like a brick.

The night had grown chilly, making Shelby wish for a jacket. Following Nash and Delaney, she walked out to his damaged Suburban parked across the street. Before Nash could assign seating arrangements, Shelby opened the back passenger door and climbed in, leaving the front passenger seat for Delaney.

"All aboard?" Nash asked, glancing back at Shelby in his rear-view mirror. "Buckle up."

Delaney had some problems getting her seatbelt fastened, so Nash leaned over and clicked it for her.

"Thanks, Nash." Her words ran together as she patted his face.

"She's really drunk," Nash said to Shelby with a chuckle.

U2 came on the radio, and Delaney reached over for the volume, cranked it up, and proceeded to sing at the top of her lungs about a beautiful day, while dancing in her seat.

Mercifully, by the time the song ended, they'd arrived at the nearby apartment complex where she and Delaney lived.

"Can you help me get her to bed?" Nash asked.

"Um, sure." Odd request if he was planning to make a move on Delaney.

While Nash guided a wobbly Delaney toward the bedroom, Shelby walked ahead and pulled back the covers for her friend. After sitting Delaney down on the bed, Nash picked up her feet, slipped off her stilettos, then laid her in bed and adjusted her legs.

"You're suth a nithe guy, Nath." No sooner did her head hit the pillow than she was out.

"Okay. Well, guess I'll head over to my place." Shelby said after pulling the covers up over Delaney's prone form.

"I'll follow you out."

"No. It's okay." She waved him off. "You can stay if you want."

"Stay?" His eyebrows shot up in confusion. "Why would I stay?"

"I—Oh, never mind." Embarrassed by her less-than-charitable thoughts about Nash, she turned to leave.

"You should probably unbutton and unzip her jeans." Nash pointed in the direction of Delaney's waist.

"What?" Shelby stopped short and stared at him like he'd just asked her to join them for a threesome.

"Those jeans are awfully tight. Might not be a good idea for her to sleep all, you know, bound up. Bad for the circulation."

"Oh." Right. Why else would he ask?

Nash turned his back, while Shelby lifted Delaney's blouse and did as he'd suggested.

"I don't know how much good she'll be to Sam tomorrow. She's going to have one hell of a tequila headache," he said as Shelby moved to the front door, with him right behind her.

He turned the lock on the front door knob, making sure Delaney was locked in for the night, then closed the door behind him.

Shelby had her apartment door unlocked and the door open just as he stepped up behind her.

"Shelby." He placed his hands on her shoulders. "You know I don't take advantage of inebriated women. Besides, I'm not attracted to Delaney," he continued, his breath warm on her ear, and she shivered in response. "You're cold. I should let you go in." He released her, leaving her bereft.

"Thanks for bringing us home, Nash." She didn't turn around. She couldn't look into those blue eyes and not make a fool of herself. She'd already done plenty of that today. The resentment she'd been harboring all these years crumbled like a dry biscuit.

"See you tomorrow night." She heard his footsteps along the sidewalk.

Tomorrow night. Stepping into her apartment, she closed the door and laid her forehead against it. Her fears had been confirmed. Coming home had been a bad idea.

4

———

If Nash never looked at another tux, it would be too soon.

Waiting in the bar for the ladies to join them, he took a healthy pull on his craft beer and eyed Ethan like he'd grown another head. Since when had his best friend become such a clothes horse?

They'd looked at tuxes with shawl lapels, notched lapels, and peaked lapels. They'd looked at dinner jackets and morning coats, cummerbunds and vests, bow ties and long ties. And still hadn't selected anything because Ethan wanted Sam's opinion and approval. He pressed a thumb to his twitching eye. Who knew there were so many choices?

Ethan caught his gaze, chuckled, and slapped him on the shoulder. "Too much?"

"No. In fact, let's go look at a few more. I'm sure we missed something in the thousands of tuxedos we looked at today."

"Just wait, my friend. One day, this will be you again."

Not. In. This. Lifetime. Been there, done that. Burned the T-shirt.

Nash had been engaged to his college sweetheart, Stephanie Cummings. It was a match made for a romantic chick-flick: he the star quarterback, she the beautiful cheerleader and homecoming queen.

And they'd been the NFL's perfect couple too.

Or so he'd thought. But Stephanie had only been interested in his star status. When he'd retired early from the NFL, she'd called in an audible, and left him for a teammate.

"You fellows looking for dates?" Sam asked as she wrapped her arms around Ethan's waist. He leaned down to kiss her and came away with a big-ass grin.

Nash nodded a greeting to Delaney. "You're alive."

"Yeah. It was touch and go there for a while," she muttered, then ordered a club soda with lime from the bartender.

Nash's gaze found Shelby, who stood off to the side like she was the fifth wheel. Her hair was back in the ponytail he remembered, and she wore what looked like a simple knit dress in deep green and a pair of flats. She'd never been one for the latest fashions, probably because growing up she hadn't had that luxury. But he liked that about her. Shelby's lack of materialism was the polar opposite of Stephanie.

"What would you like to drink?" he asked, gathering her into the huddle.

"What you're having looks good."

"Another Drafty Kilt," Nash said to the bartender.

"Drafty Kilt?" Shelby raised a brow and looked down at Nash's well-worn jeans. And damned if that look didn't stir a little heat.

"Kilt's at the cleaners," he said with a shrug, taking the glass from the bartender and handing it to Shelby. Their hands touched, lingered over the glass, and Nash had an inexplicable urge to twine his fingers through hers and bring her hand to his lips.

Even when she was out with friends, she carried a haunted look in her eyes. He found himself wanting to make that look a thing of the past. To bring back the Shelby he'd known before she'd taken life's many hits.

"Did you look at as many dresses as we looked at tuxes today?"

"That depends. We looked at approximately eight-point-four million dresses. You?"

"About the same number of tuxes. I lost count at eight million three hundred ninety-five thousand." He drained his glass. "I thought Sam had her dress picked out."

"Me too. But she said she needed to make sure she made the right decision," Shelby said with a shrug and an eye roll.

Sam filled Ethan in on their day, while Delaney nursed her nonalcoholic beverage.

The bar in the trendy new restaurant had become more crowded, the patrons pushing him and Shelby closer together until they were hip-to-hip. Someone bumped Shelby from behind, causing her to make full-frontal body contact with Nash. Breasts to chest, good parts to good parts. Shelby's mouth opened, and a flush tinted her cheeks, as he stared into her startled amber eyes.

Holy hard-on, Batman. He stepped back as if electro-cuted, bumping into the guy behind him, who shot him a dirty look.

"Quinn, party of five, your table's ready," the hostess called over the din in the bar.

Thank God for small favors, Nash thought.

~

"Man, am I tired," Delaney yawned heavily then eyed the others at the table. She nudged Sam in the chair next to her. "Aren't you exhausted?"

Sam gave her a funny look, glanced at Shelby and Nash, and then said, "Oh. Yeah. I am a little weary." She in turn gave Ethan a nudge. "How about you, babe? You tired."

With a glance at the two of them, and a furrow between his brows, he finally said, "Sure. I'm tired too," and then appeared to wait for some instruction.

They'd already divvied up the check, using Shelby's computational skills, and were just hanging out.

Delaney jumped up, grabbing her monster purse. "Great. I mean, wow, look at us turning into lightweights." She turned to Shelby and Nash. "But we don't want to rush you two." She poked first Sam and then Ethan. "Do we?"

Taking the not-so-subtle hint, Ethan stood and pulled out Sam's chair.

"Oh, but—" Shelby stood.

Placing her hands on Shelby's shoulders, Delaney pressed her back down in her seat. "No, no. Don't get up. We'll see ourselves out." With that she shooed Sam and Ethan ahead of her.

"What was that all about?" Shelby asked, totally confused.

Nash smirked. "I can only guess. Anyway, it looks like I'm driving you home."

"But it's so odd. Delaney and I live right next door to each other," Shelby insisted. "It's illogical to go home in different cars, not to mention inconvenient for both you and Ethan." She chewed on her lip, worried he would think she'd set this up. "God, Nash. I'm so sorry."

"Shelby, Sterling isn't that big. Besides, I live southeast of town. It's on my way. You ready?"

"Uh, sure." With no choice, other than a budget-breaking taxi ride, she rose from her chair and gathered her handbag.

Nash followed her out, his hand on the small of her back, warm and protective. She recalled the feel of his body against hers when she'd been pushed into him. His lean, hard body.

And now she had a nearly two-hour ride back with him all alone in a dark car. The man who'd unapologetically broken her heart. And yet, she couldn't stay away from him.

NASH HAD CARRIED the conversation while he'd made his way out of the congested Buckhead area, chatting about the sports teams he remembered Shelby following, where some of their classmates were now, and how she'd liked living in, first, New England, then California, after growing up in Sterling. But about fifteen minutes outside of Atlanta, Shelby finally spoke without being spoken to.

"You said you lived southeast of town. I thought that was mostly rural still."

"It is. I bought the old Brooks' place." He had the remaining ten acres of what had been a hundred-thirty-acre farm, but on it sat the sprawling white farmhouse and barn. He kept a couple of horses, a rescued jackass named Duke, and a barn cat. One of these days he'd add a golden retriever or two to the menagerie.

"That house must be at least ninety years old," Shelby said.

"Ninety-two to be exact, and, yeah, it needed some work. I spent the first six months having the plumbing and electrical brought up to code and putting in modern kitchen and bathroom facilities."

Shelby laughed.

"What?"

"You. It needed *some* work, but it took six months on electrical and plumbing alone." She shook her head. "Sounds like it needed a *lot* of work."

He laughed and shook his head. "You're right. It needed a shitload of work. But it turned out nice. You should come see it sometime." Stephanie would have hated the house. Too old-fashioned and welcoming. Which made him love it all the more.

"In fact, I'm having a cookout at the farm on Monday. Mostly my coaching staff and their wives and kids, but there will be some people there you know, like Sam and Ethan, Delaney . . . oh, and Grady. You remember Grady Morgan? We were in social studies together? He's my special teams coach. He married Amanda Gibson—she graduated a year behind us."

Shelby glanced his way, the reluctance on her face lit by the Suburban's interior lighting. "Thanks. Can I let you know?"

"Sure."

They rode in silence for a few miles.

"What made you return to Sterling?" Shelby finally asked.

Nash thought about it a minute. He thought about his dad, alone since his mother died three years ago, and his father's health problems. He thought about Ethan. They'd stayed in touch throughout Nash's college and NFL careers. Ethan even made it to a few games. "Family. Friends. The job. And I guess I never stopped thinking about the town. It's a great place to live."

"Yeah, I guess," Shelby muttered noncommittally.

He didn't know if she was ready to go there, but he asked anyway. "And what about you? Why did *you* return to Sterling?"

How was she supposed to answer that? To run from her mistakes? To lick her wounds? To get as far away as possible from her ex-husband and still live on the same continent? Because it's small enough to hide away from her small-knit research community? All of the above?

But, of course, she knew the answer: It was because Sterling University was the only academic institution willing to give her a job after the scandal involving her husband's research misconduct. She owed Ethan big time for that.

"Oh, you know, you can take the girl out of Sterling, but you can't take Sterling out of the girl." She laughed, and it sounded false to her ears.

"Well, Sterling is glad to have you back," Nash said with a quick look her way, his eyes warm in the vehicle's dim interior.

Her heart squeezed.

She couldn't go there again. Not with anyone, and especially not with him.

She leaned her head back, closed her eyes. Maybe if she pretended to be asleep the polite conversation would end.

She didn't want to go too far down the road of whys. The fact that her career was in shambles wasn't a big secret, but her role in the downfall was, and she'd like to keep it that way for as long as possible.

"I'll see you to your door." Nash's voice startled her in

the quiet confines of the car. She must have fallen asleep in earnest.

"Oh, you don't have to do that." She unfastened her seatbelt.

"I'd like to just the same," he said as he opened his door.

Shelby walked up to her apartment, Nash by her side, his stride relaxed.

She unlocked her door.

"Shelby?"

"Yes?" She turned to find him close, so close she could feel his warmth.

Without answering, he gazed into her eyes, then lifted his hand to cup her cheek. Nash was going to kiss her, she thought. But she couldn't let him. Yet like Mowgli falling under the snake Kaa's spell in the *Jungle Book*, she couldn't move. And the resentment she'd been trying her best to hold onto dissipated like fog on a sunny morning.

Nash leaned in, his gaze dropping to her lips, which had suddenly gone dry. Then his lips caressed hers, soft and gentle, their warmth welcome in the cool night air. A whimper rose in her throat just as his mouth released hers.

"I've wanted to do that since you backed into me in the faculty parking lot."

"You have?"

He nodded and licked his lips, as if he wanted to taste her again, and it was the sexiest thing she'd ever seen. Her knees, already weakened by his kiss, threatened to give way.

He dropped his hand from her face and took a step back.

"I hope to see you on Monday. I'm firing up the grill around noon."

"I'll let you know."

"Goodnight, Sassafras."

She had to laugh at her old nickname, even as her lips still burned from his kiss. And her heart still ached for his unrequited love.

5

―――――

Late Sunday afternoon, Nash pulled up in the driveway of his modest childhood home. Not much had changed in the years after he left for college, and then for the NFL. Since his mother died three years ago, the colorful profusion of flowers was absent from the beds. Just shrubs flanked the house now, tidy and trimmed thanks to the monthly lawn maintenance Nash paid for.

His dad couldn't keep up with the house anymore, but he refused to move into an apartment, so Nash hired out for necessary repairs, painting, housekeeping, and lawn care.

Many wondered why the son of a former NFL quarterback would grow up in a three-bedroom, two-bath brick house in a lower middle class neighborhood rather than one of the mansions in the wealthier neighborhood of Sterling Hills.

Easy. Bad investments and reckless business decisions.

Sighing, Nash gripped the steering wheel, wondering what version of Carl he would get today.

He climbed out of his SUV then reached in the backseat

for the bag of groceries he'd bought. Steaks for grilling, potatoes for baking, and ingredients for a simple salad. Man-food—his dad's favorite.

Juggling the bag, he inserted a key into the lock on the front door, calling out as he entered, "Dad, it's Nash."

Nothing.

The house was dark, the blinds closed, making the interior particularly dim after the bright sunshine outside.

"Dad?" He made his way to the back of the house and into the kitchen. "Jesus." The house was a mess, clothes strewn about, and in the kitchen, dirty dishes filled the sink. An open loaf of Wonder Bread sat on the counter, along with an empty Coca-Cola bottle and a knife with what looked like dried mayonnaise on it.

Clearly the once-a-week housekeeper wasn't enough.

Swearing under his breath, he cleared a space for the bag, then opening the fridge and peered in. Practically empty. Looked like another trip to Piggly Wiggly was in his immediate future.

He heard a toilet flush and then the sound of shuffling feet along the laminate floor. "Who's here?"

"Dad, it's Nash."

His father rounded the corner, looking unkempt in a dirty T-shirt and boxer shorts, at least two days' growth of beard covering his face.

But when a smile lit his father's expression, it tugged at Nash's heart.

"I brought steaks, potatoes, and salad for dinner. You hungry?"

Carl rubbed his once-flat belly. "I could eat."

"Good. Why don't you go shower while I clean up in here?" He opened the dishwasher to find a box of cereal.

Scrubbing his hand over his face, he held back a groan. "Dad, cereal goes in the pantry."

Confusion skittered across Carl's stubbled face. "Right."

Nash carried the cereal over to the pantry and was pleased to see that there was food on the shelves. "Why is the house such a mess? Didn't Carlotta come yesterday?"

"I fired that girl."

"Fired?" Nash spun to face his father. "Why'd you do that?"

His expression turned belligerent. "She was stealing."

"Dad, she was doing no such thing." Nash strode over and turned on the faucet then began rinsing the dirty dishes. With dried food stubbornly stuck on the dishes, it'd be a miracle if they came clean.

"She was. I can't find my pocket knife. And the other day the TV remote went missing."

"Dad, why would she steal a TV remote?" More likely his father put the knife and the remote somewhere it didn't belong, like the cereal in the dishwasher. Throwing a dishtowel over his shoulder, he filled the dishwasher, then put a detergent pod in, and turned it on.

"Who knows why that woman does what she does?"

"All right. Go shower, and when you come back out I'll have dinner going." Nash knew that arguing with his father was useless. He'd likely forget this conversation as soon as he got in the shower.

He'd have to make it up to Carlotta and beg her to come back. She'd been the only housekeeper willing to put up with his father's behavior. Her grandmother had Alzheimer's, so the actions of his father were not foreign to her.

His father shuffled back down the hall, and a few minutes later Nash heard the water come on.

Scrubbing the potatoes, he shook his head thinking about how to deal with his dad.

Carl had been a decent quarterback in the NFL, back when the players weren't paid nearly as much. A second-round draft pick with the Miami Dolphins before Nash was born, Carl later signed with the Atlanta Falcons. They moved back to Sterling, his parents' hometown.

Nash put the steaks in a Ziploc along with some marinade, then placed them in the refrigerator.

At only forty-five, his father began showing signs of what they'd thought was early-onset Alzheimer's but now believed was chronic traumatic encephalopathy, or CTE. Now fifty-six, his father's dementia-like symptoms had become more frequent and more noticeable.

Although CTE could not be definitively diagnosed until after death, as many hits as his father took, Nash and the specialist at Cornell felt almost certain that's what it was.

It's one of the reasons Nash left the NFL after his own grade three concussion and why he was so determined to find a new career and move on. He didn't want to follow in his dad's footsteps.

Potatoes in the oven, Nash went out to the back patio to start the charcoals.

He gazed out at the dilapidated tree house while he waited for the coals to heat up.

During the off-season, when Nash was eight years old, his father had built the tree house. Carl was a skilled woodworker, having grown up the son of a carpenter. But one day while Carl was working on the tree house, he'd been distracted—no one knew why or by what—and he'd sliced off two middle fingers from his throwing hand with a radial saw.

Career over.

After spreading out the coals, Nash covered the grill and went back to the kitchen to check the steaks and prepare the salad.

Nash's father had been planning for retirement from his NFL career but never expected it to end so abruptly. Sort of like what had happened with Nash.

When Nash was about three, his father bought into a car dealership in Atlanta that went belly-up due to poor management. Then he invested in a tech company that went down when the dot-com bubble burst. His parents had been lucky the house was paid off, or else they might have lost it.

After his career-ending accident, his father struggled with depression. He'd lost his identity and hadn't known what to do next. It wasn't until the aging owner of a thriving hardware store in Sterling put it on the market that Carl found his answer.

Carl loved do-it-yourself projects, despite the radial saw accident, so the hardware store was a natural choice for him, and he was very successful for the first five years. But life had a funny way of sacking you behind the line of scrimmage.

He began experiencing debilitating headaches and forgetfulness. One day, when Nash was in high school, Dink's Corner Drugs called Nash's mom and told her Carl was in the store but that he was confused about where he was.

He'd finally had to sell off the hardware store when Nash's mom became ill. His mother's eventual death had exacerbated his father's symptoms. If Nash's career hadn't ended when it did, he would have worked with his agent to move to the Falcons, where he'd be closer to home.

Nash sliced tomatoes, cucumbers, and onions for the salad then tossed some croutons in. Carrying the bowl to the kitchen table, along with a couple of dressing choices, he heard the squeaky closet door in his father's bedroom open and close. Carl should be out any minute. Time to put the steaks on.

He was just turning the steaks on the grill when the sliding glass door opened and his father stepped out wearing a haphazardly buttoned Hawaiian shirt, a pair of dress pants, one black shoe, and one brown shoe, his thick salt-and-pepper hair sticking up at odd angles like he'd toweled it off but hadn't combed it.

Heaving a sigh, Nash knew he needed to be honest with himself. It might be time to hire a full-time caregiver.

ON LABOR DAY MORNING, after feeding and watering the equines, Nash set about preparations for the cookout. Ethan would be over later to help move the picnic tables beneath the shade of a heritage live oak behind the house.

In the meantime, Nash had already hauled the steel drum smoker out from the barn and started the coals. On the menu was sweet Silver Queen corn on the cob, barbecue ribs and chicken, and hamburgers and hot dogs for the kids. Guests were bringing everything from coleslaw and potato salad to chocolate cake and peach cobbler.

The cornhole board, horseshoes, and *bocce* ball awaited kids and adults alike for some friendly competition, while Duke the Donkey could be counted on to take some of the kids for a short ride around the paddock.

As he hoisted a couple of two-hundred-quart coolers into the back of his SUV and filled them with ice from the bags he'd bought in town, he thought about Shelby and the goodnight kiss he'd been unable to resist. He nestled beer, sodas, and bottled water in the ice, along with a few bottles of white wine, while remembering the taste of her lips, the little whimper she'd let out when he'd retreated, and the way she'd looked into his eyes, as if he had just opened a door that had been bolted shut for far too long.

It had certainly unbolted a door for him. One that was probably better off closed and locked.

He still hadn't heard from her. He didn't know if she'd accept his invitation or not, but he hoped so. He wanted to see her again. Probably more than he should.

Clearly she had a lot going on and probably didn't need any further complications in her life. But he wanted to be her friend, to remind her that he's had her back since her first day of fourth grade and that he always would. Despite her notions to the contrary.

SHELBY FOUND herself driving along County Road Fifty-Seven headed to the old Brooks Farm. She'd been working on a research idea, reviewing some articles, but nothing was gelling, and she was beginning to think her ex-husband's work had been the only vehicle for her research.

She hadn't intended to accept Nash's invitation, but she couldn't take the four walls of her apartment any longer.

Nash had broken her heart, and if she wasn't careful, he'd do it again, but she couldn't make herself stay away from him. Neither could she bring herself to hold a grudge —not where Nash was concerned.

She snorted and wondered if her heart could get any more broken than it already was. Her experience with Charlie had left it in tatters. Or was it just her pride that had taken the hit?

Unsure what was on the menu at Nash's, she'd stopped at the Piggly Wiggly and picked up the fixings for a tossed salad. It would go with anything, and she could put it together when she got to the house. And as far as the cost of ingredients went, it was fairly cheap. An important factor when she was scraping the bottom of her back account.

Drawing a deep breath, Shelby rounded the bend in the road right before the turn-off to the farm. As she turned in, she noted the concrete that covered the once-red clay drive. When she arrived at the house, she counted at least ten cars and pickup trucks parked out front on the lawn.

The house wore a gleaming coat of white paint, and the glossy black shutters stood out in the midday sun. The red-brick chimneys still flanked either end of the house. Beneath a wraparound porch, black rockers beckoned for someone to come and set them in motion. A black swing on one end of the porch faced the front yard. Four lacy Boston ferns hung along the porch, their bright green leaves adding a welcome pop of color to the black and white setting.

The house looked better than she'd ever seen it.

Climbing out of the car, she gazed up at a sky so blue it almost hurt. With temperatures in the mid-seventies, it was a perfect day for one last summer barbecue. Grabbing the bags out of her back seat, she glanced down at her khaki skirt and Keds and wished for a pair of cowboy boots instead.

After picking her way across the yard and around the house to the sound of laughter and the tantalizing aroma of grilling meat, she stopped dead in her tracks when she saw the crowd. She hadn't expected so many people. Just as she considered sneaking away, Nash called her name, waving her over.

Painting a smile on her face, she headed in his direction.

She felt as if all activity had stopped and every eye was on her. Judging. All seeing her for the failure that she was. And a snitch. She rolled her eyes at the ridiculous self-centered notion, as if everyone's life revolved around hers.

"Hi. I didn't think you would come." Nash met her with a broad smile on his handsome face and relieved her of the grocery bags.

"I couldn't stand my own company anymore. I hope salad is okay."

Nash glanced in the bags. "Looks great."

Delaney waved at her, inviting her to take the empty Adirondack chair next to her.

"I'll just go get a big bowl, a knife, and a cutting board and be right back," Nash said. "Grab a drink and make yourself comfortable."

THE ADULTS WERE SPRAWLED in various places beneath the oak tree, some in chairs, some on blankets, while the kids burned off their excess energy with games of chase and dodge ball. Nash glanced around and found Shelby, Sam, and Delaney huddled around an iPad. No doubt the wedding playbook.

Ethan and a few of the coaching staff were battling it out in a game of horseshoes, while some of the coaches' wives laughed over the cornhole board.

What was left of the feast waited on the picnic tables for those with hollow legs who wanted seconds.

Rising from her seat, Shelby headed over to one of the coolers and plucked a diet soda from the icy water. Nash walked over to join her, just as Grady did the same.

"So, Shelby, you doing okay?" Grady asked as he popped

the tab on a Coke. "I heard about your divorce. That's rough."

Ah, dammit.

Shelby's face went white. Grady was a nice guy, but sometimes he didn't have the sense God gave a goose, to borrow a phrase from his late mother.

Before she could answer, Nash said, "Hey, Grady, your boy's calling you." Not a lie. His son, Mikey, was calling his dad to come watch him ride Duke.

"Oh, thanks, man. You let me or Amanda know if you need anything," he said to Shelby as he headed over to the paddock.

Shelby stood, her face a mask of shame.

"Sorry about that. Grady didn't mean anything by it."

She shook her head. "I know. You'd think I'd get used to it by now. I mean, it's not like divorce is uncommon. And in a town the size of Sterling, it's bound to get out." She bit her lip then took a sip of her soda as an afterthought.

"Come take a walk." He headed for the paddock on the other side of the barn. Some time away to compose herself would do her good and Shelby had always loved horses. Nash recalled that she had even worked at Sterling's riding stables in high school. A breeze kicked up, sending her sweet lemon fragrance his way. She looked adorable in a skirt that showed off her still-toned legs.

When they reached the fence railing, Whisky nickered and sidled over, hoping for a carrot or half an apple. Nash held out one of the carrots he'd swiped from the bag Shelby had brought, and the horse snuffled Nash's hand before crunching down on the carrot.

"This is Whisky. And that shy little girl over there is Moonshine."

"They're beautiful. I didn't know you wanted horses."

"Neither did I." He chuckled. "They sort of came with the property." He reached up to rub Whisky's muzzle. "Duke came later." He pointed to the jackass in the neighboring paddock. "Want to see if we can coax Miss Moonshine over for a carrot?"

Shelby smiled, and his heart rolled over in his chest. "Sure."

Nash handed her the carrot, and Shelby clucked to the horse.

Whisky nudged his head in, and Nash pushed him away. "No, dude. You've already had yours."

Feelings hurt, Whisky turned with a flick of his tail and wandered over to the shade of a tree.

Shelby's patience paid off when Moonshine ambled over and hung her head over the rail. She held out her hand and Moonshine took the carrot. While the horse crunched on the treat, Shelby stroked her muzzle. "Yeah, you're a sweet girl, aren't you?"

This was the most relaxed he'd seen Shelby since she'd come home. She'd lost the haunted look and had bright spots of color in her cheeks. And he had a thought. "If you'd like to come out and ride, let me know. You can saddle her up yourself, or we can ride together, either way."

Her hand paused on the horse's muzzle, and she dipped her head, a soft smile on her lips. "Thanks. I might do that."

Well, that was progress.

6

———

The following Wednesday afternoon, Nash reached over for his cup of coffee as he reviewed the previous night's practice video. With the short week, he was beginning to regret giving his guys the Labor Day Weekend off. In the three days off, his defensive line forgot how to run a zone defense, his offensive line forgot how to block, and his QB forgot how to execute a screen play.

All his players were wicked-smart—the future generation of brain surgeons and rocket scientists. College wasn't just a stepping-stone to the NFL for his guys. In fact, few, if any, were headed for a career in the NFL, but they had heart. They played for the love of the game.

Good thing, since this afternoon's practice was going to be a bitch.

His phone chirped with an incoming text. Glancing over and seeing Shelby's name, he picked it up.

I'D LIKE TO TAKE YOU UP ON YOUR OFFER.

His offer? Oh, yeah, his offer. For a second there his mind had darted into the gutter.

He texted her back.

Feel free. The tack is in the room to your right after you walk into the barn.

Damn. He'd love to join her, but that was an impossibility right now.

His phone chirped again.

Thanks.

He snorted. Guess that meant he wasn't invited anyway.

"Hey, Coach. Got a minute?" Matt, his QB coach asked.

"Sure. Come on in." He set aside his phone and turned his attention to Trent.

It was after nine o'clock that night before Nash pulled up in front of his house. He walked out to the barn to make sure the horses were secure for the night. Whisky, Moonshine, and Duke were ensconced in their stalls with fresh oats in their buckets. Moonshine's coat showed signs of recent currying. Shelby hadn't forgotten everything she'd learned working at the riding stables.

He hoped she'd had a good ride.

"Goodnight, equines."

He was bone weary as he walked to the back door of the house. On the stoop sat a container of chocolate chip cookies with a note inside. "Thanks for the therapy session."

Biting into the gooey cookie, Nash smiled. *Therapy session.* He liked it.

On Saturday morning, Shelby answered the knock on her front door to see Delaney standing there, reusable grocery bags in hand. Careful to pull the door to so Delaney couldn't see inside the apartment, she stepped out onto the stoop.

"Hey. Sam, Ethan, and I are going to tonight's football game. Want to join?"

Shelby had been planning to go, if only for the first half, to see Nash in action.

"Sure." She really enjoyed being with Delaney. She was always so cheerful and confident, as if she felt good in her own skin, a feeling Shelby used to know herself. Maybe she could reclaim that feeling again one day.

"Great. We're meeting at Ruby's for an early dinner, then we'll head over. You up for that?"

Shelby smiled at Delaney's enthusiasm. "Of course."

"See you at five-thirty," Delaney said as she headed to her car.

Later that afternoon, after another frustrating day of literature reviews, Shelby gathered a light jacket just in time for Delaney's knock. Making sure she had her faculty ID, which would get her in the game for free, she opened the door.

"You look great," Delaney said with a bright smile. "Walking okay with you? We'll never find a parking spot in town."

"Walking sounds good. I've been sitting all day." Shelby locked up and fell alongside Delaney, all decked-out in team apparel. Shelby needed to hit the university's bookstore for some Bobcats apparel. As soon as she found some spare change, that is. She'd unearthed a Bobcats-red shirt. That would have to do for now.

She still hadn't furnished her apartment. She had the bare necessities: a used kitchen table that doubled as her desk, a mattress and box spring—on the floor—and a book-shelf. For kitchen basics, she'd raided the small storage unit her mom still kept in town after moving to Miami with her new husband.

She owed her divorce attorney money. Then there was the attorney she'd hired during Stanford's research misconduct investigation. And, of course, Nash's car repairs—not to mention her own. At this rate, she might have everything paid off by the time she retired. That is, if she could afford to retire.

"What are you researching?" Delaney asked, interrupting her morose thoughts.

Shelby huffed out a laugh. "Right now I'm researching what to research."

"Oh." Delaney smiled. "Been there, done that, bought the T-shirt."

Delaney pointed to Shelby's car. "Haven't gotten that fixed yet?"

"Oh. No. It's no big deal."

"But, you have duct tape holding up your bumper."

Shelby shrugged, hoping Delaney would drop the subject. "It works for now."

They turned onto Main Street and could hear the marching band up ahead.

"So, what was it like growing up in Sterling?" Delaney asked.

"It was nice, especially after meeting Nash and Ethan." She and her single mom had moved to Sterling from Memphis the summer before fourth grade. She knew her mom had escaped an abusive relationship but never thought to ask what had brought her to a small college town in northeast Georgia.

Delaney gave her a shoulder nudge. "Tell me about it. I love a good story."

"Oh, the three of us ran wild as kids, especially in the

summer. Riding bikes, climbing trees, collecting bugs—all the things kids do in a small town—from sun up to sun down." And because her mom waited tables on the weekends at Ruby's Diner, in addition to her regular job in one of the quarry offices during the week, Shelby often found herself invited to eat with Nash or Ethan's family.

Nash and Ethan lived two doors down from one another. Shelby and her single mom, on the other hand, lived one street over in one of the duplexes in a rundown neighborhood.

"You're such a brainiac. I don't see you catching frogs and skipping rocks."

"Well, when I wasn't running the woods and streets of Sterling, you could find me curled up with a book or solving math and logic puzzles." Shelby shrugged. "I've always had a knack for numbers."

"Clearly," Delaney said with a laugh.

She and Delaney merged with more fans on their way to the university's stadium, some already rowdy from too much alcohol.

Although a tomboy, Shelby hadn't played organized sports growing up like Nash or Ethan because her mom couldn't afford it. But she'd always gone to Ethan's baseball games and Nash's football games, cheering them on all through Little League and Pop Warner, middle school and high school, and keeping stats on their performances for fun.

Their friendship sustained Shelby through the tough times, like when her mom lost her job at the diner and finances got even tighter than they already were, or when she came down with pneumonia and had to be hospitalized.

But one day, when Shelby was fifteen, her relationship with Nash had changed.

She and Nash had been climbing one of the ancient oak trees down by the abandoned gristmill when she'd slipped and landed flat on her back, knocking the wind out of her.

As she lay writhing in agony, trying to get her stunned lungs to draw in a breath, Nash jumped down from the tree and ran to her.

He'd leaned over her, and she looked up into his concerned blue eyes, and that was it. She fell, and she fell hard. Harder than her fall from the tree.

He lifted her to a sitting position. "Relax, Sassafras. Don't panic. You just got the wind knocked out of you. Hurts like hell, but you'll be fine in a minute."

Shelby coughed, painful and hard.

"That's good. Coughing is good. Means your diaphragm is working again." He knelt in front of her. "Sit up on your knees. That's it. Coach says to breathe in through your nose and out through your mouth. That's it. Good." All the while, he ran his hands up and down her back.

She drew in a deep and painful, but head-clearing, breath.

"Anything broken?" he asked as he checked her arms, wrists, and ankles.

She just shook her head no, too mesmerized by his touch to speak.

"Damn, Sassafras. You were lucky. A fall like that should have broken something." He pressed his forehead to hers and gazed into her eyes, and she held the breath just moments before she'd been grateful to take. Was he going to kiss her?

"Come on." He sat back on his heels and held his hands out to her. "Up you go."

From that moment on, Shelby Wentworth had an unrequited crush on Nash Taylor, town football hero.

"You and the guys were good buddies then?" Delaney asked, dragging Shelby back onto Main Street from her walk down Memory Lane.

"Yeah, you could say that." Shelby smiled at the memories.

"Still are from the looks of things."

"Well, things have changed, of course, with Ethan getting married, and Nash . . . Well, it's been a while."

"I don't think that matters to him," she said as she waved to some friends.

"What do you mean?"

"I mean the way he looks at you. Like he'd run through fire to protect you."

Shelby shook her head. She used to think that too. "That's just Nash. He'd run through fire to protect just about anyone."

"Maybe, but for you, he'd run through fire, brimstone, and straight into Hell."

Shelby didn't say anything.

They'd arrived at the fan-packed Ruby's and spotted Ethan and Sam.

"You know, Shelby," Delaney gave her another gentle shoulder nudge, "if you ever want to talk about it, I'm here. And Sam too."

Were her feelings for Nash that transparent? Shelby shook her head. "Thanks, though."

It was standing room only when Nash walked into McGinty's later that night. Amid claps on the back and offers to buy him drinks, he made his way to the bar, where people stood three deep. Like the Dallas Cowboys' offense opening a hole for Emmitt Smith, the crowd parted, giving him a clear path.

"What'll it be, Coach?" Hugh, McGinty's owner asked in his deep, booming voice.

"I'll take that amber ale you've got on tap."

Hugh drew the beer and handed Nash a frosty mug. "On the house. Congrats on pulling out a win."

Yeah, by the seat of his pants. He didn't know how the team managed it, but he'd take the win. "Cheers." He raised his mug to the crowd and took a satisfying pull. As he scanned the crowd, his gaze landed on Shelby sitting in the corner with his other running buddies.

She laughed at something Delaney said then tucked a stray strand of hair behind her ear. She'd begun to look more relaxed, losing some of the haunted look in her eyes.

She'd also begun to let down her guard a little more around him. Maybe she'd forgiven him after all.

He should just finish his beer and head home. Well past midnight, it had been a hell of a long day—game days always were—and a hot shower and comfortable bed sounded good. But he found himself making a beeline straight for Shelby.

As he approached the table, Shelby glanced up, and her eyes locked with his. And something clicked, just like it always did when he looked at her. The eleven years apart had done nothing to change that.

"Hey, Coach," Delaney yelled. "Come sit down." She pulled Shelby's arm, indicating she should slide over.

"Great win tonight, man!" Ethan said as he raised his glass in salute.

Nash collapsed onto the bench next to Shelby and felt that *zing* when they touched. She snapped to attention and scooted closer to Delaney, who gave her a look like, WTF?

He couldn't resist. Leaning over, he said, "Hi, Sassafras," right in Shelby's ear and noted her slight shiver in response.

What the hell was he doing? It must have been the adrenalin of a close win. Shelby wasn't the kind of woman a man toyed with. Shelby was for keeps.

"That play at the end of the third quarter . . . brilliant! Just brilliant!" Ethan said, before shoving a fry in his face. "And gutsy. That could have gone south quick."

"Yeah. Thanks." Nash reached over and stole a fry off Ethan's plate and received a kick under the table for his trouble.

No sooner had he sat down than Shelby tapped him on the arm indicating she needed to get up.

He watched her wend her way through the inebriated Bobcats fans on her way to the ladies' room, catching a glimpse of that sweet little ass in her snug blue jeans just before the crowd swallowed her up.

He drained his beer, and it took him two seconds to make up his mind to follow her.

"Where you going?" Delaney shouted above the din. "You just got here."

"I'll be back."

SHELBY WALKED OUT OF THE LADIES' room determined to go back to the table and say her goodnights. Despite her protests to the contrary, she was hungry and didn't want to spend money on food at McGinty's. She'd ordered water to drink while everyone else had beer or liquor. She'd just go home and curl up in bed with a late-night bowl of Cheerios. Dark Chocolate Crunch. Even a broke girl had to have *some* creature comforts.

Rounding the corner, she ran right into a hard immovable object. Nash Taylor.

"Whoa!" He grabbed her shoulders to keep her from falling.

"Nash!" She stepped back out of his reach. "I'm sorry, I didn't see you."

"No harm done."

She stood there for a moment, silent and awkward.

"Want to dance?"

Her gaze shot to Nash's face. "What?" The music wasn't that loud in the hallway they were standing in, but she was sure she'd misheard him.

"You know, shake our booties to the beat?"

Nope. She'd heard him correctly. Why would he ask her to dance when any one of the star-struck female Bobcats fans would gladly oblige? She shook her head. "I think you've had one too many. Besides, I was just leaving."

"I'll walk you home then."

"No. That's okay. Then you'd have to come back for your car."

"I parked in front of your apartment." He shrugged. "It was the only place I could find a spot."

"I'll be fine. You just got here anyway." She started to walk away.

"Shelby, you knew my mom. She'd tan my hide if she knew I'd let a pretty young woman walk home late at night by herself. Especially with these rowdy fans."

He thought she was pretty? She couldn't remember the last time anyone paid her a compliment, especially on her looks.

"Fine," she said with a sigh. "I'll just go say goodbye."

She felt Nash's hand on the small of her back as he

guided her through the sea of red and blue Bobcats fans in various stages of inebriation.

"I'm walking Shelby home," Nash shouted, before she could speak.

"Sure," Delaney replied with a grin. "Ethan will make sure I get home okay, right, Ethan?"

"Uh, yeah. I mean, of course." Ethan responded after Sam nudged him.

Nash followed Shelby out as she stepped into the chilly night air. Fall had finally come to north Georgia.

"You didn't bring a jacket?"

"No. It was warm when we left for the game."

He slipped off his red Bobcats jacket and draped it over her shoulders. She shivered as the warmth enveloped her, and she barely resisted putting her nose to the fabric and inhaling deeply. "Thanks," she muttered. So much for avoiding Nash. "I noticed you had your car repaired. If you send me the bill, I'll pay you back." Somehow. She could always sell her eggs.

"Forget it."

"But—"

"Forget it." This time the edge in his voice made her comply.

Students whooped and hollered. The frat parties didn't show any signs of letting up anytime soon. Clearly, Sterling loved its victories. As if college students needed a reason to party.

"You did great out there tonight." Shelby said as she and Nash strolled side-by-side along the sidewalk. Watching Nash coach had been like watching a maestro conduct an orchestra.

"Thanks. There was a point in the third quarter when I didn't think we were going to come back."

They'd been deep in their own territory with fourth and short. "And then the flea flicker."

He nodded and smiled. "And then the flea flicker." His smile could light up the night, Shelby thought.

This was bad. So, so bad.

"It got the crowd back into the game and gave us the kick in the pants we needed to pull out the win."

"Fourth and short conversions have a sixty-three percent success rate, so you were right to go for it. Not enough coaches do."

Nash stopped, looked at her like she'd just revealed the opponents' secret playbook, and then laughed.

"How do you know that?"

She stuck out her hand. "Shelby Wentworth, sports fan and numbers junkie. Nice to meet you."

He took her hand, and Shelby realized her mistake as warmth spread up her arm and across her chest. His gaze captured hers and held here pinned to the spot.

Closing the distance, Nash lifted her hand to his chest and lowered his head to kiss her. And she wanted him to. God, how she wanted him to.

"Look out!" Nash grabbed her shoulders and pulled her against him just as a guy on a skateboard flew past her, knocking her purse off her shoulder.

"Sorry, dude!" the kid yelled without looking back.

"Idiot," Nash muttered. "You okay?"

The tension between them grew as he stared into her eyes, his mouth just inches from hers. "Yeah." Shelby stepped back, breaking the spell, then they both bent down to pick up her bag and knocked heads.

"Ow!"

"Shit!"

Rubbing their foreheads, they both started laughing.

Deep, belly-shaking laughter. It felt so good. So damn good. Cathartic. Powerful. And long overdue.

Now her stomach hurt along with her head, but she'd take it. Glancing around, she realized they were only yards away from her apartment. Holding out her hand to warn him off, she bent over again and scooped up her purse.

"Thanks for walking me home, Nash." She handed him his jacket.

"Anytime, Sassafras."

With reluctant feet, she turned in the direction of her front door. It was for the best. The last thing she needed was to fall for Nash Taylor. Again. But then again, it may already be too late.

7

———

Early the next morning, Nash heard a car pulling up in front of the house. Coffee cup in hand, he walked to the front window in time to see Shelby climb out of her car and head for the barn.

Hmm. Well, he had issued her an open invitation to come out and ride whenever she wanted. Good to see she was taking him up on it.

She looked sexy in those snug jeans, but he frowned over her athletic shoes. She needed a good pair of boots to ride in, he thought.

It was a beautiful morning, cool with a hint of coming fall, and a ride sounded appealing.

He'd scheduled the post-game review for later that afternoon to allow his coaches to spend Sunday morning with their families.

Making up his mind, Nash strode through the house, stopped by the kitchen, dropped off his coffee mug, and grabbed a jacket as he passed through the mudroom and out the back door.

When he reached the barn, Shelby had just draped Moonshine's saddle blanket across her back.

"Want some company?"

Shelby gasped and spun to face him, her hand over her heart.

"Sorry about that," Nash said with a grin. "Didn't mean to startle you."

"As my mother would say, you took ten years off my life."

He noted her accent was making a comeback and he liked it. "Well, I do live here, you know."

She returned her attention to Moonshine, adjusted her bridle. "I wouldn't mind some company," she said, her voice so soft he wasn't sure he'd heard her correctly.

"Great. How about we ride over to Pine Bough Creek?" He, Ethan, and Shelby used to swim in the creek in the heat of summer, clothes and all. He remembered the summer Shelby turned sixteen and the way her thin white tank top had done little to conceal her hard nipples when she'd waded out of the water. He and Ethan had talked about that for months on end.

He'd wanted her even then. But he and Ethan had made a pact in sixth grade that Shelby was off limits to both of them. They'd spit and shook on it, and you didn't break promises made with that most sacred of rituals.

He'd held up his end of the bargain, even though years later it had meant hurting Shelby.

"Sure. Although I don't think we'll be swimming today." She slung the saddle up over Moonshine's back and cinched the strap.

Yeah. Too bad.

He smiled over the shared memories. The years between them fell away whenever they were together. They just seemed to pick up wherever they'd left off. And since they left off with him crushing on Shelby and not being able to have her, it wasn't necessarily a good place to pick up again.

SHELBY TOOK a deep breath of the fresh country air, relaxed and contented, if only for the moment, with Nash by her side. Country living suited him.

He'd made something out of his life, and when adversity had taken him away from the game he loved, he'd shifted gears and found another career that allowed him to stay with the sport. She admired that.

She knew she needed to do the same, but knowing and doing were two different things.

"Let's stop here," he said as he dismounted in a sunny patch alongside the lazy creek.

She followed suit, releasing Moonshine's reins so she could graze alongside Whisky.

Nash stretched out on the ground, plucked a late dandelion, and handed it to Shelby as she sat next to him. "Thanks." She smiled at the sweet gesture she remembered from childhood, and tucked the flower behind her ear.

Whisky nickered, then settled beneath a shady tree.

Leaning back on her hands, she crossed one ankle over the other. "God, I missed this place. I didn't realize how much until just now."

"I know what you mean. The things we took for granted as kids mean so much more now."

That might be true of some things, but she'd never taken Nash for granted.

Shelby lay back in the grass, lifted her face to the sun, and closed her eyes, listening to the breeze in the trees, the call of a cardinal, and the breathing of the man next to her. She'd missed more things than Pine Bough Creek.

She felt his gaze on her face, and the heat of embarrassment competed with the heat of the sun. Opening her eyes, she turned to face him. "What are you looking at?"

"You."

A butterfly fluttered in her stomach. How long had she wanted this? How long had she yearned for Nash's notice of her as someone other than a friend?

Rising up on his elbow, he leaned over her, his gaze intense as he lifted his free hand to cup her face, and her heart battered her ribs. "Stop me, Shelby. Tell me no."

"No."

He dropped his hand.

"No." Against her better judgment, she rose to meet him. "I meant, no, I don't want you to stop. I don't want to tell you no."

HE GROANED low in his throat then pulled her beneath him as his mouth took hers. Her lips were warm from the sunshine, and her sweet lemon scent engulfed him.

Her fingers found their way into his hair, stroking, gripping, and he wanted more. So much more.

Their tongues danced, dipping and swaying. He nibbled her lip, reveled in her indrawn breath. He swept a hand along her ribs, the heat of her conjuring images of her in his bed, naked and willing.

Sweet Jesus.

He broke the kiss, nipped his way along her jaw to her ear, sucking her earlobe into his mouth. Gasping, she turned her head, giving him easier access to the tender skin on her neck. He could feel her erratic pulse when he pressed his lips to her, his pulse just as erratic.

When she wrapped a leg around him, he was lost. Lost in the feel, the smell, the taste of her. His fingers found the buttons on her blouse, opening them until he could slip his hand inside. She arched against his hand as he cupped her breast, his thumb working the pebbled peak.

Her breath hitched, her hands glided over his back, and he shifted his weight, settling between her hips, moaning when his erection pressed against her center. If he didn't stop this right now, they'd be naked in no time, for anyone who came along to see. And Shelby deserved better than that.

Calling on a reserve of will power he hadn't needed since the days of NFL training camp, he broke the kiss and rolled off her. "We can't. Not here."

Her brow furrowed, and she raised a shaking hand to her wet, swollen lips. Sitting up, she looked around as if just now aware of her surroundings.

"Come home with me?" His voice was rough with desire. She nodded.

Pulling her up by her outstretched hand, he then buttoned up her blouse and adjusted her jacket before sending her off to Moonshine with a pat on her butt.

Adjusting himself, he winced. Nothing like a horseback ride with a hard on. But if Shelby welcomed him at the other end of the ride, it would be worth it.

THEY WERE silent on the ride back, giving Shelby some time and space to think about what they'd almost done. God, she wanted Nash. Wanted him in a way the teenage Shelby never could. Wanted him with her heart, her head, and her body.

They watered and fed the horses, and Nash released them into the paddock.

She should leave. She should get in her car, start driving, and never look back. Because this had disaster written all over it.

Nash clasped her hand in his and she caved. "How about something to drink?"

She nodded and headed toward the house with him by her side.

In the kitchen, Nash pulled two bottles of water from the fridge, opened one, and handed it to her, before opening his own.

Her mouth had gone desert dry, and not from the ride. She gulped two swallows before setting the bottle on the granite counter behind her. He followed suit. Then backed her up against that same counter, his blue eyes locked on hers.

"God, Shelby. I know your life is complicated right now, and I don't want to add anymore complications." He skimmed a finger along her cheekbone, and she closed her eyes, leaning into his caress.

"But?"

"But I want you more than I've ever wanted another woman in my life. It's selfish and short-sighted, but there it is."

Her knees trembled, and she suddenly forgot how to breathe.

"Tell me you want me too."

She nodded, the only thing she was capable of at the moment.

He smelled like hay and horses and fresh sweat. He

tilted his head, his mouth honed in on hers, and the anticipation of his kiss nearly made her drop to her knees. And when his mouth found hers, she felt as if she were coming home.

Capturing her mouth with his, she reveled in the warmth and sweetness. His hands gripped her hips, and his tongue slipped between her lips to tangle with hers. Visions of him hovering over by the creek flooded her brain. The feel of his hard body, the heat of him nestled against her, spurred her on as his mouth continued to plunder hers.

Her hands glided along his shoulders, skimmed along his neck, before she plunged her fingers into his hair.

Sliding his hand down her ribs, she was struck anew by how large his hands were, and she shivered at the thought of those hands on the rest of her body.

His hands brushed her breasts, and she arched to meet them. He undid the buttons on her blouse until he could peel it back. Lifting her, he sat her up on the counter. The feel of ice-cold water cut through the haze of her desire, and as water spilled across the counter and down the cabinets onto the floor, the spike in her adrenalin had nothing to do with arousal, and everything to do with fear.

"Oh my god, I'm so sorry."

Nash almost laughed until he saw the look in her eyes. Fear.

She jumped off the counter and made a grab for the roll of paper towels next to the sink, while also pulling her blouse closed.

"Shelby. Shelby. It's okay. It's just water." He took the roll from her hands, set it on the counter. "And besides, it was my fault. I'm the one who set you on the counter."

"I should have put the cap back on the bottle. I wasn't thinking." Her hands fluttered, looking for something to do. He caught them, held them to his chest. "You couldn't have known."

She shook her head.

He had a sick feeling in the pit of his stomach.

"Shelby, what's this all about? What are you afraid of?"

Moving away from him, she bit her lip and looked away.

His smartphone rang.

Sweet Jesus! Talk about poor timing.

He pulled the phone from his back pocket, glanced at the screen, and stalked into the living room. "This better be important."

"Uh, Coach?" his assistant stammered on the other end of the line.

"Kenny, what the hell do you want? I gave you the morning off."

"I've got the game films ready for you. You said you wanted to come in and review them before the post-game review meeting today."

Nash scrubbed his hands down his face. "Right." He looked down at the bulge in his jeans. "Just load them on the computer and I'll be in later."

"Right, Coach."

Sending his gaze heavenward, he groaned and hung up the phone.

When he walked back into the kitchen, he found Shelby, her hair rumpled, her lips swollen, and her eyes wide. She'd misbuttoned her blouse, and her jeans were wet from the water she'd spilled.

Damn. Guess she was leaving.

"I have to go. We shouldn't be doing this anyway." She strode toward the front door.

"Dammit, Shelby. Don't leave like this." He followed her to the living room.

The closing of the door was the only sound that met his plea.

HER FINGERS GRIPPED the steering wheel as she sped along Country Road Fifty-Seven back toward town. She never should have come out. She never should have accepted his invitation to ride.

The spilled water brought bitter memories flooding back. The time Charlie yelled at her for knocking the bottle of water over on his laptop. Never mind that she hadn't left an opened bottle of water next to a valuable computer—it had been him—but she'd taken the blame. Or the time he berated her in front of their grad assistants when she came in late for a meeting after getting sick in the bathroom from food poisoning.

But, bad memories aside, she should be grateful she'd knocked over the water. It had stopped what couldn't happen. She knew that if she slept with Nash there'd be no going back. At least for her.

It wouldn't be just sex for her. It would be the beginning of the end for her heart.

8

———

That afternoon, Nash and his coaches gathered in the media room to view the tapes from the previous night's game, cups of coffee at their elbows.

Some had writing pads and pens at hand, others electronic tablets, but they all took notes as they dissected the game, play-by-play. Nash tried to refocus his attention after his morning with Shelby and his suspicions about her ex-husband, but the look on her face when she'd left was like a helmet-to-helmet hit. It left him aching for her.

"Grady, work on Hansen's blocking," Nash said, using a laser pointer to indicate the missed block.

"Already noted, Coach."

Nash cringed on the next play when Angelo, their QB, got sacked. "Kevin, what the hell was Drew doing on that play?"

The offensive coordinator, Kevin, shook his head. "We'll work on it, Coach."

Nash's smartphone rang. Normally, he would've ignored

it, but it was his dad. He held up a finger to his staff, indicating he needed to take the call.

"Dad, I'm in post-game. What do you need?"

"Nash? Is that you?"

"Yeah, Dad. *You* called *me*. What's up?"

His father hesitated. "I, uh, I don't remember."

"Okay, well, I'll come by later—"

"No, wait! I remember. There's someone in the attic."

"Dad, there's no one in the attic. Remember? I checked it the other day." Nash could feel the eyes of his staff on him. He rose from his chair and walked over to the corner of the room, turning his back.

"Son, I heard them walking around. They're probably robbing me blind as we speak!"

"Dad, listen." Nash lowered his voice. "No one can get in the attic in the first place, much less steal what's stored up there." When he'd checked the other day, he'd been surprised by all the crap—broken small appliances, old football pads and cleats (his and his dad's), boxes of yearbooks, and other high school paraphernalia.

"Well, I can't sit here and do nothing! I'm going up there to run whoever it is off!"

"No. Dad!" Dammit. He'd hung up. Drawing in a deep breath, he turned back to the group then gave them a stiff smile. "I need to go check on my dad. Kevin, can you take it from here?"

"Sure, Coach."

Avoiding the concerned expressions on everyone's faces, Nash gathered his iPad and keys. "I'll call you later."

Then he got the hell out of Dodge.

WALKING past McGinty's on the way to the local drug store on the Monday after her close call with Nash, Shelby spotted a sign in the window. HELP WANTED. WAIT-STAFF AND BARTENDER.

After paying bills and balancing her checkbook that morning, she had just enough money left to buy some feminine necessities like Midol, Tampax, and a pint of Ben & Jerry's Chocolate Fudge Brownie.

Thinking of her ever-insufficient checking account balance and her maxed-out credit cards, she considered the job. She'd waited tables in a respectable restaurant in Providence while she attended Brown University. Thinking of her mom's years as a waitress, she guessed maybe it was in her blood.

She gnawed on her lower lip. But could she bear the stigma of waiting tables at McGinty's, knowing she would be waiting on former high school classmates, her students, even her academic colleagues?

Maybe she should look for something in one of the neighboring towns, somewhere she'd be less likely to see people she knew. She had to do something. Soon. She hadn't been this deep in debt since she'd been a college student.

"Hey, Shelby."

She turned to see Delaney. Even in jeans and a T-shirt, Delaney looked like a walking sexpot.

"Hi, Delaney."

"You thinking about lunch?" She pointed to McGinty's. "I was just thinking about grabbing a quick bite. Want to join?"

Considering her lack of funds, her answer had to be no. *Dammit.* She liked Delaney and wouldn't mind getting to know her a little better. Holding back a groan of regret, she scrounged for an excuse. "Thanks, but I have an appointment. Maybe some other time."

"Sure." Delaney's understanding smile added to Shelby's disappointment.

"I'd better go." Shelby pointed in the direction of the drug store.

"See you later then." Delaney waved as she opened the door of McGinty's.

Even more depressed now than she was when she set out on her mission, she wondered if she had enough to buy *two* pints of Ben & Jerry's.

Monday evening, Nash stood in the medication aisle of the Piggly Wiggly trying to decide which laxative to get for his father. "Too many damn choices," he muttered. Not to mention embarrassing as hell. Buying Stephanie's Tampax was less humiliating. At least anyone who saw would know they weren't for him. He needed to make a decision before someone saw him.

"Hey, Nash."

Too late. He groaned then pasted a smile on his face and turned to greet Delaney.

"Hi, Delaney."

They chatted a few minutes about the football season, a typical conversation when he ran into folks around town.

"By the way, I ran into Shelby earlier today outside McGinty's."

"That's nice," he replied, still too preoccupied with his escape. Not from Delaney—he really liked her—from his present predicament.

"She was looking at the want ad they had in the window for wait staff."

That got his attention. "Wait. What?"

"Yeah. She acted all nonchalant, but when I asked her to lunch she said she had to run."

"Well, maybe she had something going on." Nash said, waving off her speculation.

"Maybe. But did you know she still hasn't had her car fixed?"

He frowned. He hadn't seen the backend of her car. "Maybe she hasn't had the time to drive up to Carlyle."

"That, or she can't afford to have it fixed."

Nash put his free hand on his hip. "What are you saying, Delaney? That Shelby is having financial problems?"

"I think so. She's looking at a want ad, her bumper is duct-taped to her car, after the first football game, she didn't order anything to eat from McGinty's—"

"Maybe she wasn't hungry."

Shelby leveled him with a look. "She didn't order anything after the football game. Not even a soda. Just water. It all adds up."

Nash considered Delaney's observations. If it was true, Nash new that Shelby would never ask for help. She'd grown up wearing hand-me-downs and eating Hamburger Helper. She wouldn't want to admit she was still living hand-to-mouth.

But she had a good job, so how could that be?

He nodded. But he didn't know what he or Delaney could do about it. It wasn't as if she'd take charity.

"What should we do?" Delaney asked, her eyes filled with concern.

Delaney wore her heart on her sleeve most of the time. It was one of the things he admired about her.

"I don't know, but I'll give it some thought."

"Good. Let me know if I can help."

"Will do."

"Oh, and if you're looking for a laxative, magnesium citrate works best. My grandfather swears by it," she said with a wink.

Juuust shoot me. Nash thought his dilemma had gone unnoticed. The joys of living in a small town.

NASH TURNED into his driveway the following Wednesday. It was only four twenty, and he should've gone back to his office at the stadium, but after spending the afternoon with his dad at a doctor's appointment, he knew he wouldn't be able to concentrate on work.

The results of his dad's neuro-psych tests were getting worse. Today he couldn't remember his address or phone number.

He spotted Shelby's still-damaged car parked in the driveway and was reminded of Delaney's concerns. Nash had been mulling over a plan, but he'd been preoccupied with his father's continued decline. He had a few more issues to iron out, and then he'd set the plan in motion.

But still, he couldn't understand how a professor—even an assistant professor—could be that strapped. But whatever the reason, he'd always stood by Shelby and would continue to stand by her when she needed him, even if she wouldn't admit it.

For now, he just wanted to get to the bottom of Shelby's reaction to the spilled water the other day.

Entering the house, he grabbed a couple of beers from

the fridge and walked back out onto the porch, settling himself in the swing.

Moments later, Shelby picked her way across the lawn toward her car, jacket slung over her shoulder.

"Want a beer?" He held up the second bottle.

She stopped, hesitated, then glanced his way. "I'm sorry to disturb you. I didn't think you'd be home this early."

"You're not disturbing me, Shelby." God, he hated seeing her like this. Cowed. Unsure of herself. And of him. "Come on. One beer."

She turned her feet in the direction of the porch, and he couldn't help but smile.

Handing her the beer, he patted the swing. "Go for a swing, Sassafras?"

She shook her head, laughed, then sat down next to him, and he pushed the swing back and let it go.

While she took a swig of her beer, he asked how her ride was.

"Good. I rode over to the old gristmill. It's a shame to see it so dilapidated. Someone needs to buy it and give it some tender loving care." She eyed him over her bottle.

"Oh, no you don't. I'm fresh out of tender loving care after fixing up this money pit," he said as he gestured toward the house with his bottle of beer.

They sat in companionable silence for a few minutes, both lost in thought. Or memories.

"Hey." Nash broke the silence. "Remember when you, Ethan, and I used to play Truth or Dare?"

Shelby nodded, then laughed.

"The silly questions we used to ask? 'If you were a superhero, who would you be?' or the dares like 'Ring Mrs. Colburn's door and run?' How about a game now?"

"You offered me a beer to play Truth or Dare?"

At her reluctance, Nash prodded, "Come on. Where's the Shelby who used to give as good as she got?"

She wouldn't look at him, so he gave her shoulder a nudge. "Truth or dare?"

She waited a beat then said, "Truth."

"All right. If you had to pick the all-time best NFL quarterback who would it be?"

Her gaze shot to his face. Clearly not the question she'd expected.

"You already know."

"You can't say me," he said with a grin.

She snorted. "Wasn't going to."

"Ouch." He rubbed the imaginary wound on his chest.

"Peyton Manning."

"You just think he's cute," Nash teased.

"Hey. Five hundred thirty-nine career touchdowns for a total of over seventy-one thousand yards and a completion percentage of sixty-five-point-three."

"Fine." He threw his hand up in surrender. "Your turn."

"Truth or dare?"

"Truth."

"Did you toilet paper the Kaminsky's yard senior year?"

He laughed. "Yes."

"You sneak! And you didn't invite me?"

"It was past your curfew. Your mom would have tanned your hide."

"That's no excuse."

Still grinning, he asked, "Truth or dare?"

"Truth."

He dropped the grin and looked Shelby in the eye. "Did he hurt you?" he asked, his voice rough with emotion.

She sucked in a breath, and he thought he'd pushed too

hard too fast. Shelby shook her head, picking at the label on her beer. "No. At least not physically."

He fisted his free hand by his side. If he ever encountered her ex-husband, he'd make sure he never hurt Shelby again. Physically or otherwise.

"Okay. Then how?"

She turned her head, her arms wrapped around her, and looked out at the setting sun, gnawing on her lip.

"Talk to me Shelby," Nash entreated her, his voice gentle.

She nodded, hands clinched in a fist. "You have to understand. Charles Ingram was a god in the world of statistics. When I learned he would be my dissertation chair and that I would get to work as his grad assistant, well, it would have been like you being able to train under Tom Brady or Roger Staubach—"

"Or Peyton Manning."

A smile ghosted across her face. "Yeah." The smile evaporated, and she rubbed her arms as if cold. "He was the reason I went to Stanford. We started seeing each other outside of work. He invited me to meetings with researchers who were the rock stars of their fields. I was in awe of him and his friends. One thing led to another, and the next thing I knew we were married."

"But after I married him it went downhill. We argued if I wanted to go out with friends or colleagues. Then he always had some reason why I couldn't fly home to see my mom or why she couldn't come to see me."

"Separating you from friends and family," Nash muttered.

"His control began so slowly that I hardly noticed my transition from a confident, strong young woman to a . . . doormat. He would berate me in front of our grad students, in front of other researchers." She threw up her hand as if in defeat. "I got so tired of fighting that I stopped standing up for myself. I backed down when he pressed me."

"So, the spilled water . . ."

"Yeah. He would have yelled at me, called me clumsy, or worse, stupid."

He set his beer on the ground and took her by the shoulders. A tear trickled down her cheek. "You are light years from stupid, and don't let him or anyone else make you think otherwise. You just need to get your mojo back."

"Right. I'll work on that." She took another pull on her beer.

Taking her free hand, he clasped it in his. "Seriously, Shelby. Don't let that asshole get the better of you. He isn't worth it."

Maybe it was his pep talk, maybe it was the beer, but he saw a little spark in Shelby's eyes. "Truth or dare?" she asked.

He smiled, "Dare."

"Kiss me."

9

Nash felt those words all the way down to his groin. He cupped Shelby's beautiful face then gently wiped the tear from her cheek with the pad of his thumb. Her asshole ex-husband didn't know what he'd had. Her gaze flickered to his lips, lingering there, and he felt himself grow hard.

Taking her hand, he pulled her up and walked to the front door and into the living room. His house was secluded, but he didn't want to risk someone driving up and seeing them. And if this went where he hoped it would, the swing was no place for it.

He gently pushed her down on the couch and covered her, rocking into her and feeling the rush of adrenalin when she moaned at the contact.

Making quick work of the buttons, he opened her blouse then caressed her hard nipples through her bra, eliciting a throaty moan from her. She wore a simple black bra, no lace, no bows. So Shelby. But seeing her pale skin in contrast with the black of her bra made him groan with desire.

Flicking open the front closure of her bra with one hand, he smoothed his other hand along her inner thigh.

When her breasts were bare before him, he devoured her with his gaze. "So beautiful," he whispered. How he'd resisted her all through high school, he'd never know. But he damned sure couldn't resist her any longer. Ever since the interlude by the creek, Shelby had been on his mind.

He had to touch and taste her. Taking a nipple into his mouth, he traced it with his tongue, and he felt a shudder ripple through her. Offering the same treatment to her other breast, his fingers grazed the silky soft skin of her stomach before dipping beneath the waistband of her jeans.

"Oh God, Nash." With her breathy pants and his own labored breathing, they sounded like two horny teenagers making out on his parents' couch. And he loved it! He couldn't remember the last time he'd just made out with a woman.

The house phone rang. *What the hell?*

"Do you need to get that?" she asked in a breathy pant.

"No. Ignore it."

It rang five times then stopped. Now, back to business, he thought. Then it started ringing again. Thinking about his dad, he got up to answer it.

"Oh, for the love of—whoever it is, you're dead meat," he growled as he rose, adjusted himself, and stalked into the kitchen.

"Nash," he ground out.

"Hiya, Coach! Catch you at a bad time?"

Nash bit back an expletive. "What is it Grady?"

"You asked me to let you know when the new tackling dummies arrived, so I'm letting you know."

Closing his eyes, he ground his teeth. "Good to know,

Grady. I'll see them tomorrow." He hung up without waiting for a reply.

When he walked back into the living room, Shelby was sitting up on the couch and had gathered her blouse around her.

"Sorry about that. Good news is my employees do what I ask. Bad news is my employees do what I ask." He didn't know what to do or how to recreate the mood. And he wanted to. God, how he wanted to.

Her gaze landed on his crotch, and she licked her lips. His gut clenched as he held in the groan of desire waiting for some signal from her.

"Truth or dare?" Shelby asked as she lifted her eyes to his face, her cheeks flushed.

Intrigued, he said, "Dare."

"Take me to bed."

That would be the signal. Her request stunned him, but he quickly recovered. "I thought you'd never ask."

Rising, she wrapped her arms around his neck, kissed him, timid and shy at first. He let her lead the dance. Then she gave him a gentle shove, and he fell back onto the couch. When she climbed onto his lap, he almost cried hallelujah.

She deepened the kiss. Turning up the heat, she straddled him as her hands got busy on his fly. Before she could get too far in her endeavors, he wrapped his hands around her thighs and stood up, walking with her to his room and his king-size bed.

Gently lying her on the mattress, he followed her down, covering her. She rocked her hips into him, sending molten heat straight to his already-overheated parts.

Wasting little time, he flicked open her bra again. "Now, where were we? Oh, yes. I believe we were right here," he murmured as his tongue grazed first one nipple then the other.

SHELBY GASPED when his mouth claimed her breast, his dark skin and stubble in stark contrast to her own pale skin.

Warning bells sounded in her head.

Then his hand slid between her legs, cupping her, and she didn't care. The house could fall down around them, and as long as he was touching her, she wouldn't have noticed. She'd been waiting for what felt like her whole life for this.

"I want to see you, Shelby," he whispered. Undoing the button on her jeans, he pressed a kiss to her stomach, and she arched into him. As he slid the zipper down, his lips followed until he met the top of her panties.

Rising, he pulled her jeans off, taking her panties with them, then stood looking down at her, his heated gaze sweeping across her like fire across a dry plain.

There was no shyness, no shame. He made her feel like the most beautiful woman in the world.

"My imagination doesn't hold a candle to the reality."

His imagination? He'd imagined her naked? She'd imagined him naked too, and she couldn't wait another minute for her reality.

"Your turn." She stood up and ran her hands beneath his T-shirt, along his smooth skin. The muscles of his stomach quivered at her touch. Lifting the hem, she pulled the shirt over his head, standing on tiptoes to reach. Then she stepped back to admire the treasure she'd uncovered.

"Shelby, you keep looking at me like that, and this won't last long."

She smiled. She felt wicked and . . . free. Sex with Charlie hadn't exactly been the stuff of fantasy, and it only got worse as the years passed.

Reaching out, she flicked open his unbuttoned fly and reached in to take him in her hand.

"Je-sus!"

Latching on to her wrists, he pulled her hand free and stepped out of his jeans. He was a work of art. Lean muscles, broad shoulders, hard flat stomach. She wanted to kiss every inch of him.

"No," he said as if he'd read her mind. "Not yet."

He gave her a gentle shove, and she fell back onto the mattress. Making his way up her body, he kissed her inner thighs, her stomach, her breasts, as she writhed in both agony and ecstasy.

His fingers caressed her thigh before giving her what she craved.

Her hips rose to meet his hand, and he took her mouth with his, his tongue stroking and swirling, mimicking the tantalizing movements of his fingers.

And then she was gone. Shattered into a million pieces.

NASH COULDN'T WAIT another second. He reached into the bedside table drawer for a condom. Hovering over her, he tore open the packet and rolled it on, then captured her mouth once more. He entered her slow and easy, clenching his jaw against the strain of holding himself in check.

That restraint didn't last, as she wrapped her legs around his waist and thrust her hips against his.

"Nash," she moaned.

"I've got you. Hold onto me." His thrusts increased,

harder and faster, hardly able to believe that he was inside Shelby at last. Something he'd fantasized about since he was a horny teenager.

Her breathy pants in his ear, he drove into her, seeking release for them both. When she took his earlobe between her teeth, he came undone. A light flashed behind his eyes, and he thrust one last time before collapsing, breathing as if he'd just run the length of a football field. Twice.

Rolling off her and onto his side, he gathered her into him, enfolding her in his arms, as their breathing returned to normal. He stroked her arm, eyes closed, reveling in the feel of her.

Drifting in a pool of contentment, he started when Shelby's voice broke the silence.

"GOD, Nash. I saw the play. The hit. I was so scared." She choked up, felt the tears in the back of her throat. She'd held her breath waiting for him to move as he lay there on the field. To give some sign of life. He'd been knocked unconscious and was still out when they'd brought the backboard and cart out to pick him up.

The sickening hit he took had made all the highlight reels and was the talk of the NFL and safety experts for months afterward.

Being with him now only reminded her how close he'd come to a devastating injury, or worse, death.

"Yeah, me too. But, I can't have regrets. I can't think about what could have been. I've got to accept things as they are and keep moving forward."

She could take a lesson from Nash on that.

She hadn't asked and felt bad that she hadn't. She closed

her eyes against the pain of her selfishness then opened her eyes and looked his way, searching his face in the fading light. "Do you have any residual issues from the concussion?"

"I get headaches, and I see a specialist up at Cornell twice a year. That's where I was when you first came back to town." He tucked an arm under his pillow. "I get cognitive function tests, neuro-psych testing, and MRIs. You know, to catch any changes in my brain."

She rolled onto her side to face him. "God, Nash. It's that bad?"

"Well, not yet. Hopefully, it never will be. But that's the point, right? To catch it before it gets bad. Not that there's a whole lot I can do about it."

They were silent a few beats, her heart battering her ribs as she thought of Nash with a neurodegenerative disorder.

"Do you miss it?" she finally asked.

He stroked her cheek. "Well, I don't miss getting hit." He grinned. "But yeah, I miss watching the perfect play unfold, the adrenalin rush when my long bomb is caught for a touchdown, the crowd noise."

"I could see how that would be addicting."

"I still get the rush, but now it's for my guys."

"I watched your press conference. You looked shell-shocked."

He snorted. "Yeah. I don't know which was worse—giving up the game I loved or standing there alone while I did it."

She lifted up on her elbow and looked down at him. "Why was that? Where was Stephanie in all this?"

∼

Nash sat up against the headboard, positioning the pillow behind his back. Shelby followed suit, pulling the blanket up to cover her breasts. Pity.

Sighing, he spoke. "She didn't bother to show up that day. No. Looking back, Stephanie had never been there for the difficult parts."

Shortly after he'd signed with the Broncos, he and Stephanie had moved to Cherry Hills Village, a suburb of Denver and one of the most affluent neighborhoods in Colorado, and he'd given her carte blanche on the house, from picking it out, to furnishing it.

She'd chosen a modern, nine thousand square-foot monstrosity of stone and glass then filled it with sleek, cold, modern furniture of chrome and more glass. Decorated it to intimidate whoever entered. Even him, so it seemed. But she had been enjoying herself, so he let her have at it.

That Stephanie didn't bother to use the degree she'd earned in social work, but chose instead to throw herself into Cherry Hills' active social life, didn't really bother him either.

He focused his energy and attention on becoming the best quarterback the Broncos had ever had, no easy feat given past QB greats like John Elway and Jake Plummer.

Wedding plans were underway for the off-season, a destination wedding on the Caribbean Island of Nevis.

Shifting to a more comfortable position, he continued, "I became friendly with another rookie on the team, Colin Jackson, wide receiver. We both came from small towns, both played for SEC schools, and both were first-round draft picks."

"I remember him. He's with the Raiders now, right?"

"Yeah. For some reason, Stephanie couldn't stand him. Whenever he'd come over for dinner or with some of the other guys for a cookout, she'd ask me why I had to invite Colin. No matter how friendly Colin tried to be, she'd give him the cold shoulder."

Other than that, Stephanie settled into life as the wife of an NFL quarterback. She sat with the other wives at the home games, had the wives over for away games, or joined them at their homes.

"After my concussion and being placed on injured reserve, Stephanie grew sullen and distant, always asking when I would be able to play again. When I decided to consult a specialist in traumatic brain injury at Cornell before making a decision, she flew off the handle. Why? Weren't the team doctors good enough? Didn't I want to start playing again as soon as possible?"

Shelby reached out and took his hand in hers. Just that small gesture spoke volumes. He had no doubt that, if Shelby had been there, she would have stood by his side at that press conference. Because that's what you did when you cared about someone.

"Dr. Ibrahim, the Cornell specialist, told me if I took another hit, even one with less impact than the one that had injured me, I could spend the rest of my life permanently disabled. Continuing to play football would've been like playing a game of Russian Roulette. It would only be a matter of time before the chamber with the bullet fired."

With the CTE symptoms his father was showing, the disease was high on Nash's radar.

The options had been clear: continue to play football and risk death or permanent disability, or leave the game he loved and live a relatively healthy life.

"So, you made the only decision you could and left the game."

With his free hand, he stroked Shelby's arm. "Too bad Stephanie didn't see it the same way."

"What did she do?" Shelby asked, laying her head on his shoulder. Nothing felt as right as they did in that moment.

"She'd been furious that I would just walk away from my career. She bailed on me." He still got angry thinking about that afternoon.

He'd come home to find suitcases by the door and her waiting for him in the cold, impersonal living room.

"She couldn't believe I had given up football. And the kicker in all this? It wasn't about the money. It was about the prestige of being Nash Taylor's wife." He snorted in disgust. "She couldn't understand why I had to walk away from all that."

Stunned by her avarice for the spotlight, if not for the money, Nash had stood and stared at the woman he'd loved. The woman he thought loved him in return, when all along she'd just loved the money and fame of being his wife. Nothing more.

"When the doorbell rang, she said it was her ride. I assumed she'd called a limo service, but when I glanced out the window, I saw a familiar car—a red Maserati Ghibli."

Shelby's brow puckered in confusion. "Whose was it?"

"Colin Jackson's." Turned out his friend's betrayal had hurt worse than his wife's.

"Oh, Nash." As she sat up on her knees to face him, the blanket fell away, leaving her bare. But the only thing he wanted to look at in that moment was Shelby's beautiful concerned face. She cupped his jaw and gazed into his eyes. "What a fool she was." Leaning in, she pressed her lips to his. His hands skimmed up her bare back then drew her into him.

Taking control of the kiss, he swept his tongue along her

lips and into her mouth, her breathy sighs a balm to his injured heart. And when she straddled him, the hurt and the anger that had lingered for the last three years fell away.

He must have dozed off because the next thing he knew he was alone. Sitting up, he looked around for evidence that this hadn't been just another fantasy. He spotted it in the form of a pair of hot pink panties lying on the floor and couldn't stop the grin that spread across his face.

A noise from the kitchen caught his attention. He got up, pulled on his jeans, and walked barefoot through the house. It was dark outside, and his stomach let him know it was dinner time.

Turning the corner into the kitchen, he caught her, bent over, head in the fridge, clearly looking for food.

In his T-shirt, her legs and feet bare, she was a sight. A sight that made him forget his hunger for food and shifted his attention toward another hunger.

He snuck up behind her and grabbed her around the waist.

Screeching, she would have collapsed if he hadn't had his arm around her.

"Jesus, Nash! You scared me!"

He buried his face in her neck and chuckled. "Who'd you think it was?" He ran a hand up her thigh to her bare bottom, enjoying the gasp his touch elicited.

"I thought you were asleep." She panted.

"I was. Got hungry." He nuzzled behind her ear and felt her shiver.

"I was trying to rectify that when you snuck up behind me and took ten years off my life."

"Yeah, well, I'm not hungry for food anymore."

She turned in his arms. "No?"

"No."

"Then what are you hungry for?" She lifted a brow in challenge.

Taking her by the waist, he lifted her onto the kitchen island. She squealed when her bare bottom hit the cold granite, and he chuckled.

"I'll show you." Opening her legs, he stepped between them and reached for the wallet still in the back pocket of his jeans. Pulling out a foil packet, he waved it in front of her eyes.

"Well, isn't that handy?" she asked, her voice heavy with sarcasm.

"I live by the Boy Scout oath." He dropped his jeans to the floor, and her hands quickly found his bare ass.

"You were never a Boy Scout." Her gaze dropped to his erection.

"Doesn't mean I'm not always prepared. Now, stop talking, woman, and kiss me."

And she gladly obliged, drawing in a breath when he entered her.

"God, Nash. You feel so good." She dropped her head back and let him take control. His big quarterback hands gripped her thighs, holding her in place as he drove into her, over and over. She felt the tension build tighter and tighter until she thought she might burst with it.

As her release washed over her, he growled in response to his own.

And on the tip of her tongue were the words, *I love you.*

～

LATER THAT NIGHT, Nash lay awake in the dark staring up at the ceiling, trying to figure out if he said or did something to make Shelby run away like her ass was on fire.

With memories of her soft skin sliding against his, his name on her lips, her hands gripping his shoulders as she came, he knew a sleepless night lay ahead.

He rolled over, and her sweet lemon scent rose from the pillow, making him groan. Part of him wanted to change the sheets, and another part of him wanted to bury his face in the pillow and breathe her in.

What the hell was he supposed to do now? He knew this wasn't enough. He wanted her again already.

What would this do to their friendship? And would Ethan sense the change?

And yet, he couldn't regret what they'd done.

He'd had the best of intentions when he'd asked her to have a beer with him. He'd been giving her situation some thought, and he had a plan in mind. Then one thing led to another, and the next thing he knew, they were naked in his bed.

So then he'd made up his mind to ask her to stay for dinner and talk with her then.

But she'd fled before he could ask.

He'd just have to find another time to present his offer. Except now that he'd taken Shelby to bed, his offer had gotten a whole lot more complicated.

10

———

The following day, Shelby pulled out of the faculty parking lot and drove along Quarry Road past the football practice field. All she had to go home to was a lonely, mostly unfurnished apartment, some leftovers, and an evening poring over want ads on Craigslist for jobs in one of the neighboring towns.

And memories of her night with Nash.

After their kitchen interlude, she'd made some excuse about papers to grade and escaped like the hounds of Hell were dogging her heels.

She knew Nash had been confused, but she couldn't help it. If she'd stayed, they would have ended up back in his bed for a fourth round, and she knew she'd never get through it without saying those three words that she'd never be able to take back.

A few people stood outside the fence watching the undefeated Bobcats practice for this weekend's upcoming trip to face Georgia Southern.

On a whim, Shelby pulled into the lot and threw the car in park.

Tapping her fingers on the steering wheel, she muttered, "Don't do it. Just turn around and go home." Since she'd fled Nash's house the night before, she'd been moping around like a lovesick teenager desperate to see him again.

Heaving a big sigh, she climbed out of the car anyway and walked over to join the other spectators. Dressed in athletic shorts and a Bobcats T-shirt and ball cap, a whistle around his neck, Nash stalked the field as his guys lined up along the line of scrimmage.

Gathering her sweater around her, she wondered how he could wear shorts on such a chilly, overcast afternoon. But she was glad he did. He had the most beautiful legs she'd ever seen on a man.

And the rest of him was pretty damned beautiful too.

Clapping his hands, he approached his starting QB and gave him a helmet slap, followed by a butt pat, then walked over to the sidelines again.

Nash Taylor in his element, Shelby thought. Watching him on the sidelines on Saturdays, anyone could see it wasn't just his love for the game or his skilled play-calling. He loved and respected his players. And clearly the feeling was mutual.

At the end of the play, he blew the whistle. "All right men, let's huddle up."

The players encircled Nash, the assistant coaches and coordinators forming the outer ring. Shelby couldn't hear what Nash was saying, but he definitely had the team's attention. A few minutes later, "Go Bobcats!" rang out, drawing applause from the onlookers. The team headed for the locker room facilities in the new ten-thousand-seat stadium across the street, a gift from a wealthy quarry owner.

Just as she turned to beat a hasty retreat, Shelby heard

her name and groaned. Turning, she saw Nash trotting over to her.

"What are you doing here?" he asked when he reached her, a grin lighting his face.

"Thought I'd stop by, see if you needed my expert opinion," she said with shrug and a smile, coming up with a quick cover.

"Funny you should say that." He tucked an iPad under his arm, adjusted his cap.

"What do you mean?"

"I mean, I could use your expert opinion."

"Okay, I think you should run it up the middle on third and short. Not only are they successful sixty-six percent of the time, they're over sixteen percent more successful than passes on third and short."

He snorted. "You may be right. Walk with me." He directed her toward the stadium and presumably his office.

"All right."

"You, uh, okay?"

She knew what he was asking, but chose to ignore it. "Sure. Why wouldn't I be?"

He laughed. "No reason." He cleared his throat and looked straight ahead. "While Sterling's football team is still in its infancy—"

"Yes, I know. You started it just three years ago, but you've done an amazing job. And look at this brand new stadium," she said, sweeping her hands out to encompass the red-brick walls of the building.

"I'm chasing the Division I FCS title this year. And I could use your help."

"I hate to disappoint you, but my kicking days are over."

He smiled, shook his head. "Maybe. I haven't seen you

kick in a while, but your statistics days aren't over, Dr. Wentworth."

"Statistics?"

"Yeah. We have a team of grad assistants collecting the stats, but we need someone with experience in analyzing them. Spotting trends. We haven't had a team statistician. Too young to have any significant stats to compare. But now we've got some meat on our bones, and I could use someone who can run the numbers—beyond the basics—on both the Bobcats and on our opponents. You know football. You know numbers. And you know what football numbers matter most, as you just demonstrated with those stats on third and short."

They'd reached his office. Unlocking the door, he flipped on the lights. "Water?" he asked as he walked over to a small fridge in the corner.

"Sure." She looked around his office. Cluttered desk against one wall, side-by-side computer monitors, abandoned coffee mug. He had a big picture window overlooking the practice field, a small sofa, a coffee table, and an end table. Bookshelves along one wall were lined with books on his sport, everything from *Football Scouting Methods* to *The Blind Side.*

She couldn't deny that his request intrigued her. She'd have to do it on the side, along with teaching her classes and finding her groove again when it came to her research.

It meant working with Nash, seeing him on a regular basis. Could her heart handle it?

It also meant no more sex. As a direct report to him, even as a volunteer, she and Nash couldn't have a romantic relationship.

Cart before the horse, Shelby. A romantic relationship

could be the farthest thing from Nash's mind. Maybe for him it was just a one-night stand.

A glass trophy case stood in the corner. In it, his Heisman Trophy, the Davy O'Brien Award, and the Maxwell Award, along with his ESPY for Best College Football Player and trophies from his high school days. His athletic superiority evident in the gleaming white marble, cast bronze, and brass statues.

He'd accomplished some impressive stats in his short NFL career. What he could have accomplished had he stayed, no one will ever know. He might have been one of the most successful quarterbacks in NFL history.

"Here." Nash came up behind her, handed her a cold bottle of water. His spicy cologne mixed with the scent of sweat for a lethal combination.

Taking the water from him, she said, "You're a natural-born coach, Nash."

"You think so?"

"I know so. I always thought that, even when you were playing Pop Warner. You always knew how to get the team fired up."

"Some days I wonder . . ." He screwed the top back on the bottle, set it aside, then put his hands on her shoulders, and her breath backed up in her throat. "What do you say? Will you be my team statistician?"

HER AMBER EYES WIDE, her lips parted. God, he wanted to kiss her. Gather her in and kiss her until they were both breathless. Her gaze went to his mouth. She wanted that kiss as much as he did.

And after last night, he knew how electric that kiss could

be. But last night had to be where it ended if she agreed to work for him.

"Coach—oh, I'm sorry, I didn't know you were, uh, with someone."

Nash dropped his hands, turned and gave Grady an eat-shit-and-die look.

Nevertheless, Grady couldn't wipe the grin off his face. Until Nash leveled him with a frosty glare that would make Hell freeze over. "I'll come back later." He turned on his heel to go, and Nash called him back.

"Yeah, Coach?"

Nash looked at Shelby, eyebrows raised in question. She nodded. "Meet our new team statistician."

Grady broke into a big grin and clapped his hands once. "Yeah? Hot damn, we got ourselves a statistician." With that he left them alone, a spring in his step, the Bobcats' fight song floating down the hall behind him.

"Now, let's talk salary—"

"Salary? But, I thought I'd just—"

"Oh, no. I'm not looking to use our . . . friendship," he didn't know what else to call it, "for the benefit of me or the team. Your time is valuable, and I intend to compensate you for that time."

"Nash—"

"No. This is nonnegotiable. You'll have to clear it with your department chair, but as Seth Durden is a huge football fan, that shouldn't be too difficult."

He threw out a number, and Shelby's mouth fell open.

"Too low?"

"No." She held up her hand. "No. That's plenty."

"Good."

He took a step back, swept his gaze over her. "Also, stop by the Sterling Bookstore and pick up some Bobcats gear—polos, sweatshirts, a jacket, and maybe a visor or ball cap. Tell them to put it on the team's account." He wanted her to feel like part of the team. He'd reimburse the school for the expense.

"This is too much."

"What's too much? If you're sitting in the booth with my offensive and defensive coordinators feeding them stats, you need to be in uniform."

"The booth?"

"Well, yeah. Where did you think you'd be?"

"But, I thought I would run the numbers, create some graphs, put together a weekly report, and that would be it. Isn't that how it usually works?"

"Yes. But you're not the usual statistician."

He pulled a book off the shelf, tossed it to her—*Moneyball: The Art of Winning an Unfair Game.*

"Did you read the book or see the movie?"

She nodded. "Both."

"Paul DePodesta was the A's secret weapon, and now you're mine."

"I don't know." She shook her head. "This is happening too fast."

"I need a statistician. You're perfect for the job. What's too fast about that?" He put an arm around her shoulder and felt the *zing* of contact. "We're going to make a great team."

STILL STUNNED by the evening's turn of events, Shelby crawled onto her mattress on the floor. Working for Nash, she'd be making over half her annual salary as a professor, and that money would go a long way to helping her pay off her debts and get back on her feet again.

That, and she knew she'd love the job.

But. Two problems.

One. She needed to focus on her research. If she had any hope of moving up to an associate professor position at Sterling, which she'd had at Stanford before the Great Career Suicide, she needed journal articles. And in order to publish journal articles, she needed to do research. And in order to do research, she needed a research hypothesis.

She'd been fresh out of those since this whole trip through Hell had started. *No one's fault but your own.* Her ex-husband's words rang in her head.

Two. She'd be in close personal contact with Nash almost daily. Which meant she'd have to hide her feelings, just like she had when they were teenagers. It also meant she'd be exposed to his warmth, his charm, and his magnetism. Which she didn't think she could resist, especially after last night.

And resist she must. A relationship with him now could cost her professorship, in addition to her part-time job with the team, and then where would she be? The position with the mathematics department had been her only lifeline. That, and her tattered heart couldn't take another blow. From any man, and certainly not from him, especially when that heart still carried the scars from his betrayal eleven years ago.

Which begged the question: Why did she sleep with him? She snorted. Not that there was any actual *sleep* involved. And she'd "slept" with him because she'd wanted to since forever.

She'd already said yes to the job, but that was when she

thought her duties would begin and end with charts and reports.

Reaching over for the notepad and pen she kept on the floor by the bed, she drew a line down the center, wrote "Pros" on one side of the line, and "Cons" on the other.

Under pros went "money," and under that she listed all the things she could do with that money. Things like "pay off attorney bills," "pay for Nash's car repairs," and, as she looked around her bedroom at the boxes on the floor and grimaced, "buy a dresser."

Under cons, she listed "time," "career," and "research." Tapping her lip with the pen, she considered other factors.

"Job satisfaction" went in the pros column. Tilting her head, she realized that was something she hadn't felt in a while, even before the GCS. Also under pros, she listed "seeing Nash regularly." This also made it onto the cons list.

Then she added the biggest con yet: No more sex with Nash.

Maybe it was for the best. It would only be a matter of time before he'd be ready to move on. At least this way she had a solid reason to avoid further intimate contact with him.

Heaving a sigh of disappointment, she reviewed the lists.

Even with the cons, the possibility that she could get herself out of debt and maybe have a little to put away swayed her decision. She could always do it for the remainder of the football season and earn the extra cash until Nash found someone permanent.

Surely she could protect her heart for three months. Right?

Remembering last night, the way he tasted, how he touched her with such tenderness, and then that moment in

Nash's office when it looked like he was about to kiss her again, she sighed. The odds were definitely not in her favor.

11

———

Removing the ringing smartphone from his pocket, Nash frowned at the caller ID. "This is Nash."

"Nash, Sheriff Cole. I, uh, I've got your dad here at the station," he said, hesitation in his voice.

"Jesus. Is he okay?"

A heavy sigh followed. "He's fine, but Nash . . . I had to arrest him."

"Son-of-a—what for?" Nash made an about-face and returned to his car. Combing his hands through his hair, he squeezed his eyes shut momentarily.

"He was removing his clothes in Mrs. Snyder's front yard."

"Damn. How far did he get before you picked him up?" Nash held his breath, dreading the answer.

"He was in his boxers and socks."

"Thank God for small favors," Nash muttered. "I'm on my way."

"Nash?"

"Yeah."

"He's pretty bad. I was thinking of calling 911."

"Don't. Thanks for calling me first."

After six hours in the ER at Sterling Regional Medical Center, then two more in the Emory University Hospital ER, where he'd requested his dad be transferred, Nash pulled into his driveway and released the death grip he'd had on the steering wheel. One o'clock in the morning.

According to the psychiatrist who'd treated his dad, his father had had a psychotic break, hearing voices telling him his clothes were on fire, and he had to take them off.

Shutting off the car, Nash scrubbed his face with both hands, a lump in his throat. Would this be him someday?

Carl was now medicated and safely ensconced in a private room. If he stabilized, he'd be discharged in a few days, which gave Nash some time to figure out what to do next.

He now had a new medication regimen, which included the anti-psychotic risperidone.

He'd need a health care worker to make sure his father followed the new plan. No way could his dad do it on his own.

Tomorrow. Right now, he needed a hot shower, and a soft bed.

ONCE SHE'D RECEIVED the approval of her dean, Shelby wasted no time in getting her feet wet. She dove into the team's stats headfirst. With just two years' worth of stats, she didn't have much depth, but she'd often worked with less.

Most university sports programs hired graduate students to collect and record game stats, while managers or equipment staff kept practice stats and videoed practice. Sterling hired six students who sat in the new stadium's press box. Two acted as spotters: one for all offensive plays for both teams, and one for all defensive plays for both teams. These spotters called out who was playing on that particular down, kept track of whether it was a pass play or a rush. On the defensive side, the spotter called out tackles, interceptions, sacks, etc.

One student served as the inputter, entering all data into a DOS program called StatCrew. In case of a computer meltdown, the team also employed a scribe, who manually kept the data the old-fashioned way—by hand. Finally, there were two participation keepers, who checked players off as they came in and out of the game.

At the end of each game, reports were generated for each team, which were then shared with each coach. Each week, before the next game, the coaches reviewed the last three box scores—the structured summary of the results of the games. Game stats were also posted to the team's website.

Part of Shelby's job would be to take over the staff books generated each week for the coaches. But she wanted to do much more than generate generic reports, and from what Nash had said, he wanted more too. She planned to analyze the data, search for trends, strengths, and weaknesses. Her goal was to gather rich data that could be analyzed to actually inform sideline decision-making.

As she pulled up StatCrew on her laptop to familiarize herself with the software—what its strengths were, what its weaknesses were—she began making notes. Her notes would help her create her own database, which she could use to run reports and perform sophisticated analyses using such methods as basic regression analysis, logistic regression, Monte Carlo simulation, classification, and hierarchical regression.

Her excitement grew. She finally felt as if she'd climbed back onto the horse that had bucked her off. And it was exhilarating.

She'd eventually tinker with her own methods, some of which she'd developed during her ill-fated career at Stanford, to answer questions about game strategy and tactics. Eventually, the data and methods could be used to develop statistical models to measure player value and forecast future performance for use in making recruiting decisions, *à la Moneyball.*

Of course, she'd mastered advanced spreadsheet skills including pivot tables, macros, scripting, and chart customization throughout her career.

If she did her job well, and she intended to, the tool could be used by future statisticians after she stepped out of the role at the end of the current season. The key was to develop a set of analyses and algorithms to run that would keep things consistent and eliminate, or at least minimize, confounding factors.

Of course, the number-cruncher had to understand the sport and the challenges coaches and players needed to overcome in order to win.

Shelby glanced at the clock, shocked to find it was already eleven-fifteen. She'd been working on this for close to four hours. She couldn't recall the last time she'd been so engrossed in her work that she lost track of time.

Rubbing the back of her neck, but satisfied with the progress she'd made on the new database, she packed it in. She had some interesting stats to include in her first staff book.

Intellectually energized for the first time in years, she smiled.

THE MONDAY after her second home game as statistician, Shelby knocked on Nash's office door.

"Yeah?" he called out, then glanced up with a smile. "Shelby. Thanks for coming by. I know you've already put in a full day."

"Sure." She couldn't figure out why Nash wanted to see her.

"Have a seat."

"Why do I feel like I've been called to the principal's office?" She tucked her hands between her knees when she sat down.

"Not at all. First things first." He pulled a large gift-wrapped box out from under his desk. "This is for you."

Shelby froze. "What's that?"

"Consider it an early birthday present," he said with a grin.

"But my birthday isn't until February."

"Okay, then it's an early Christmas gift."

"But—"

"Just open the box, Shelby."

"Fine." Taking the box, she set it on her lap and tore open the paper to reveal a Lucchese boot box. "What the—"

"If you're going to keep riding Moonshine, you at least need to wear a decent pair of boots."

She lifted the lid to see a beautiful, hand-tooled pair of boots in tan. She ran her fingers over the fine craftsmanship. She'd never owned anything so nice. "Nash, I can't—"

"Yes, you can."

Dismissing her objection, he moved on. "Now, the second reason for this meeting—you're doing a great job. I never had my doubts, but I also never expected your freakish number-crunching to have such a direct impact on the outcome of last Saturday's game."

She shrugged, still in awe of the boots, as she lifted them from the box. "It's what I do."

"And oh so well. That's why I want you to come to South Carolina next week."

She practically dropped the boot she'd been holding in her hands. Confused, yet trying to temper her excitement over what he was saying, Shelby asked, "You mean you want me to travel with the team?"

"That's exactly what I mean."

She shook her head. "But, stats people don't usually travel with the team."

"I thought we'd already determined you're not the usual stats person." He rose from his desk and came around to perch a hip on the corner. His hair was sticking up as if he'd been running his fingers through it recently. "You've proven your value to this team after just two home games. Why would I leave such a valuable commodity behind when we're off to play the Citadel, our most difficult opponent of the season?"

"And your staff? They're okay with that?"

"They are. But even if they weren't, I'm the coach, and you're just as much a part of this team as any of the other coaches."

Shelby couldn't contain her excitement a moment longer despite her reservations.

But Nash was a professional. He wouldn't let their recent encounter get in the way of his job. Or hers. In fact, he'd made no more attempts to kiss her . . . sadly.

"I'd love to travel with the team." She would be spending even more time with Nash. And despite his restraint, it was becoming increasingly difficult to keep her hands to herself. And, more importantly, rein in her heart.

~

A WEEK after beating the Citadel, Shelby gathered her purse, laptop, and keys to head over to the stadium for her meeting with Nash. She'd reviewed their upcoming opponent's stats and found some interesting weaknesses, especially their ineffectiveness against fake punts.

Just as she reached her front door, someone knocked. Peering through the peephole, she sucked in a breath. It was Nash. And he had a pizza box from Momma Michelle's in one hand and what looked like a bottle of wine in the other. What the—

"Shelby, I know you're there. Your wrecked car is still parked outside."

Chewing on her lip, she considered not answering. Maybe he'd think that she had walked or ridden a bike— never mind that she didn't have one—and give up and meet her at the stadium as planned.

"Come on, Shelby. I can practically hear you thinking."

Damn. She opened the door and stepped out like she was leaving, then closed the door behind her. "Nash. I was just on my way out to meet you. You didn't need to pick me up."

"I thought we could meet here. Quieter. More convenient for you. And I know it's a little early, but I brought dinner." He held up the pizza, which smelled like Heaven, especially since she'd skipped lunch.

"Oh, but, I thought we could use the projector in the conference room."

"Nah. Not necessary. By the way, why haven't you had your car repaired?"

"Oh, just busy."

"I see."

She stood rooted to the spot, trying to figure out something else. She couldn't let him in her apartment for two reasons. One, he'd see it was empty, and two, she couldn't be in such close quarters with him again. She worked for him now. Sex with her boss had career-suicide written all over it. Just like marrying her mentor. "Well, my apartment is a bit of a mess. I haven't really finished unpacking." Not a total lie. She was still living out of boxes, but only because she didn't have any furniture to put her things in.

"So what? Come on, I'm starved, and the pizza's getting cold."

Resigned to her fate, she opened the door and stepped aside.

Nash followed her in and stopped short. What was supposed to be the living room held boxes of her books—both academic tomes and pleasure reading—an old desktop PC sat on the floor next to a printer, and the *pièce de résistance*, a small TV sat on a TV tray.

Yep. Home sweet home.

"What the hell? You've been here how long and don't have any furniture? What happened? The moving company lose it or something?"

"Um. No." She dropped her purse on the floor by the front door and set her laptop on a box. "I don't have any furniture."

Avoiding his scrutiny, she took the pizza and wine from him and walked into the kitchen. She could really use a glass of wine about now. Thankfully, it was a screw top, since she didn't have a corkscrew.

Reaching into a cupboard, she took out two mismatched highball glasses—any port in a storm, right?—and poured some wine. Turning, she handed one to him and raised the other to her lips for a mouthful.

"Shelby, where is your furniture?" He took the glass from her and set it on the counter then put his hands on his hips.

"I left it."

"You left it where?"

"In California."

His brow furrowed in confusion. "Isn't California a community property state?"

"Yes."

"So, why?"

She turned and pulled two plates out of the cabinet where the pitiful collection of glasses were and opened the pizza box. "When I left, I just wanted out. I didn't want to haggle over . . . stuff."

"Okay, but why haven't you bought new furniture?" When his response was met with silence, he stepped up behind her and placed his hands on her shoulders. "Shelby?"

"Because I can't. I can't afford it."

~

Nash turned her toward him, her face a mask of shame and reluctance.

"Talk to me, Shelby." He held up his hand. "Wait." He took the plates, put them on top of the pizza box and carried it to the table, then went back for the wine and glasses, tore off some paper towels from the roll by the sink, and indicated she should join him at the table.

After serving them both a slice of pizza, he said, "Talk."

Shelby took another gulp of wine, which prompted Nash to say, "And eat."

She took a bite of pizza, wiped her mouth with the paper towel, and lifted her gaze to his. "I'm broke," she shrugged, "and I'm in debt."

Delaney had been right about her financial issues, but he never would have guessed how bad those issues were.

"What do you mean you're broke? What about your divorce?" He thought about the money he'd paid to his ex-wife—and *she* was the one who'd cheated—who'd walked out on their marriage. "What about your portion of the assets?"

"What assets? California is a not only a community property state, it's also a community debt state. Debts incurred by either spouse during the marriage belong equally to both spouses. And my ex ran up a lot of debt." She pushed aside her half-eaten pizza slice. "Plus, I still owe my divorce attorney money, and the attorney who represented me for the year-long research misconduct investigation."

"Jesus." He rubbed the back of his neck. "Why didn't you say something?"

"To who?"

"To me? To Ethan? Delaney?"

"And then you'd do what exactly?"

"Help you."

"No. Absolutely not." She folded her arms across her chest. "I'm not taking money from my friends." Then she waved her hand. "Besides, the money I'm making numbering-crunching for you is starting to put a dent in my debt."

"Let me—"

"No. I mean it, Nash. I'll be fine." She picked up her now-cold slice of pizza. "Can we just eat and get to work?"

Even growing up, Shelby and her mom wouldn't accept help. When her mom lost her job at the diner, he and Ethan's family had offered to help, but the answer had always been no. The best they could do was to invite Shelby to dinner as often as possible.

He didn't want to drop it, but he would for now. He couldn't bear the thought of Shelby living out of boxes with no furniture. He hoped she at least had a box spring and mattress.

He had a moment of discomfort. If Shelby knew the reason he'd given her the job, she'd be pissed. It didn't matter now, though, because while he'd only been trying to help, she'd helped him and the team instead.

After they'd finished dinner, Shelby sat next to him and opened up her laptop to display graphics, including a bar graph and a pie chart. She started rattling off an alphabet of software: SQL and R/S-PLUS, SAS and SPSS.

He had no idea what she was talking about, but he loved seeing her in her element, her amber eyes alight with excitement. Much better than the shame he'd seen in those eyes earlier.

Everything she'd said was Greek to him, but when she boiled it all down, she made it clear and understandable, taking complex statistical analyses and communicating them effectively. She must be some teacher, he thought. For a minute, he let what she said flow over him and just enjoyed watching her, his gaze drawn to her mouth. He wanted to kiss her. No, he *needed* to kiss her. Like he needed to draw his next shaky breath.

Even as she chattered on, he leaned in, until the next word froze on her lips and her gaze slid to his mouth.

"Nash, don't. We can't do this. I work for you now."

"Just one more kiss. Nothing more." He closed the distance between them, slow and easy. Then their lips touched, and she sighed into his mouth.

Need for more than just her lips against his shot through him, hot and sharp. More. He wanted . . . more. Pulling her out of her chair and into his lap, she straddled him, her fingers in his hair. Her sweet lemon scent tickled his nose as her hair fell around them.

The hell with one more kiss! Just as he stood to take her . . . somewhere, he didn't know where, since she didn't have a couch, his phone rang.

Groaning, he looked down at his phone lying on the table, then his heart filled with trepidation when he saw the number. Reaching for the phone, he accepted the call. "This is Nash."

"Mr. Taylor, this is Crystal."

She sounded like she'd been crying. He hoped his dad hadn't hurt her feelings.

"Your dad . . . he's missing."

12

———

"Missing?" The pizza congealed in his stomach. Shelby's gaze shot to his face, and she climbed off his lap. "What do you mean? How long has he been gone?"

"About half an hour. I . . . I went to the bathroom, and when I came out the front door was open, and he was not in the house."

"Shit." He looked up at Shelby and saw concern there.

"I've been looking for him and calling his name, but I can't find him anywhere."

"Okay. Listen, I'm on my way." He pressed a thumb to his right eye where a headache had begun.

"Do you want me to call 911?"

"No. I'll call the sheriff directly." He ended the call and looked into Shelby's concerned face. "My dad is missing. I have to go."

"I'm coming with you." Shelby closed her laptop and headed for the door.

"That's not necessary," he said as he followed her.

"I know it's not necessary." She pulled her smartphone out of her purse and started dialing.

"Who are you calling?"

"Delaney. You need to call Ethan and Sam. We can use everyone's help."

Nash wanted to keep this quiet. Didn't want to embarrass his dad. He'd done his best to keep his father's condition out of the media thus far.

At his hesitation, she prodded. "What's more important? Protecting your father's privacy or finding him safe?"

"Right. Call."

When they arrived at his father's house, the police were already there, cars parked on the street, lights flashing.

Sheriff Jim Cole greeted him. "All right. I've spoken to the home health aide. He's been missing now about forty-five minutes."

Ethan pulled up, and he and Sam jumped out of the car and ran over to where Nash, Shelby, and the deputies were gathered.

Jim led them over to the hood of his car where a map of the area was spread out.

"Can you think of somewhere your father might go? A favorite spot?"

Nash rubbed his forehead. "The hardware store. The high school football field. Ruby's." He shook his head. "I don't know."

"I called Ruby's. They haven't seen him," Ethan supplied.

Nash looked up. They were losing the light fast. It'd be fully dark soon. And the temperatures were dropping as fast as the light was fading.

"We'll find him, Nash." The sheriff clapped him on the shoulder. "All right." He turned to address his officers and the friends and neighbors who'd come out to help. "We all know what Carl looks like. He was wearing a pair of black sweats, tennis shoes, and a gray Atlanta Falcons T-shirt."

As Nash listened to the sheriff's instructions to the volunteers, a small, warm hand curled around his. Shelby gave his hand a squeeze and leaned into him. Her quiet support meant more to him than all the other volunteers' who stood at the ready to help.

THEY'D BEEN SEARCHING the neighborhood for over an hour, and still no sign of Nash's father. Nash and Shelby circled back to the house, partly to get an update from the sheriff, and partly to use the bathroom and get something to drink.

While Nash went to the bathroom, Shelby grabbed a couple of water bottles out of the fridge. Opening one, she wandered over to the sliding glass doors. "Where are you, Carl?" she muttered to herself. She couldn't imagine the hell Nash was going through right now. Odds were, they'd find his dad safe, if not cold and hungry. But there was always that small chance.

There were ravines in the area. Rocky ravines where she, Ethan, and Nash had played as kids. But in the dark, it would be easy to take a tumble.

A light in the backyard caught her eye—up high, at tree level—where the old tree house would be if it were still there. Her heart started pounding.

Nash joined her at the door, and she handed Nash the other bottle of water.

"Do you see that?" She pointed out the pale light.

"Holy shit. The tree house."

Yanking open the sliding glass door, he raced toward the

tree. "Dad! Carl!" He began climbing the wooden rungs bolted into the tree.

"Careful, Nash," Shelby called out as she craned her neck to watch him climb. "The wood looks pretty rotted."

She pulled out her smartphone and hit the flashlight app to help light Nash's way. He disappeared inside the tree house.

"He's here!"

She placed her hand over her racing heart. *Please let him be okay.*

She waited what seemed like a lifetime for further word.

"He's sound asleep."

"Thank God."

It took the fire department to get Carl down using a ladder. When he was back safely on the ground, he blinked at the crowd gathered around him, seemingly perplexed by the hullabaloo.

Nash, who'd been waiting impatiently for the fireman to carry Carl down, grabbed his dad by the shoulder and hauled him in for a hug. "Jesus, Dad. What were you thinking?"

"What was I thinking? Son, your mother and I have been looking for you for hours, so I went up in the tree house to see if you were hanging out with your friends."

Shelby caught Nash's pained look, and her heart ached for him.

As a fireman draped a Mylar blanket over Carl's shoulders, Nash just shook his head and led his father back into the house.

~

With the help of Crystal, Nash got his father tucked into bed. He had a few cuts on his hands where he'd apparently slipped climbing up into the tree house, but nothing serious. It definitely could have been worse. Much worse.

Crystal continued to apologize, clearly afraid she was going to lose her job. Nash did what he could to reassure her, but he didn't know what would happen tomorrow when she had to report everything to the home health agency.

He sent her home, told her to get some sleep.

Ethan, Sam, and Delaney were the last to leave after all the law enforcement, first responders, neighbors, and other volunteers had packed it in.

Just Shelby remained.

Nash collapsed on the sofa next to her and laid his head back against the cushion. "What a night." He closed his eyes for a moment, took a deep breath, then felt Shelby's hand close around his.

She'd been his rock tonight. Calm, steady, and supportive. And she'd been the one to find his father. He'd never be able to thank her enough.

Lifting his head, he brought her hand to his lips. "Thank you."

She raised her other hand to caress his cheek. "You're welcome." Then she leaned her head on his shoulder. "I'm so glad he's okay."

"Me too." He released a heavy sigh. "I think this is the sign I've been looking for."

"For what?"

He looked down at his lap, then back at her. "To make the decision to put my dad in a facility. Somewhere he'll be safe."

Shelby turned and knelt next to him, her searching gaze locked with his. "Do you think this is CTE?"

"I do. And so does Dr. Ibrahim, the specialist I see at Cornell."

"So, you retired."

"So, I retired." He scrubbed a hand over his face. "And yet, it could still be me someday."

"It could, but I think your odds are better than your father's."

"And why's that? Cause my head is harder?" He huffed out a laugh devoid of humor.

"Because you only had thirty-six college career sacks, and other than the hit that ended your career, you had the lowest sacks on record in the NFL."

He drew back. "How do you know that?"

He watched in fascination as a blush crept up her neck and into her cheeks.

She ducked her head then looked up at him, her eyes filled with . . . something. Admiration? "I kept stats on all your games."

"You did?" He couldn't have been more shocked. "Really? Why?"

She bit her lip, and God help him, but he wanted to bite that lip too.

"Shelby?"

"Because," she shrugged, "I followed your college and pro careers just like I followed your Pop Warner and high school careers."

He decided to let it go at that, but aside from being flattered, he wondered why she would have not only kept his stats, but memorized them as well.

"I should go. Let you get some sleep."

"I'll see you home."

"No. I'm fine. It's not that far. You stay here. With your

dad." She rose from the couch. "If you need anything, let me know."

"Thanks." He followed her to the door, and before she could open it, he took her by the shoulders and gazed down into her face. "Thank you, again."

"You've already said that," she said, a soft smile lifting the corners of her sweet mouth.

"I'll never be able to say it enough."

She licked her lips, and his gaze dropped to her mouth. Lowering his head, he grazed her lips, ever so soft, then retreated. "Goodnight, Shelby."

"Goodnight, Nash."

Opening the door, she walked out into the dark, chilly night. Nash couldn't help but wonder whether, if his dad hadn't gone missing, he'd be spending the night in Shelby's bed.

And violating university policy. A fireable offense.

Nash groaned when his cell phone woke him from a deep sleep. Then he sat bolt upright. Where was his dad?

Dammit! He hadn't meant to sleep so soundly. Grabbing his phone, he looked at the number. Ethan.

Accepting the call, he strode down the hall to his father's room. Still in bed asleep. Thank God.

"What's up?" Nash asked, his voice soft so as not to wake his father.

"You, uh, you have company?" Ethan asked, a chuckle in his voice.

"No." He pulled his father's door closed. "Dad's still asleep. I'd like to keep it that way for a while longer."

"Turn on ESPN News."

"Don't tell me."

"Afraid so," Ethan confirmed.

"How the hell?" Nash pointed the remote at the TV, then selected ESPN.

ESPN's anchor spoke, a photo of his dad in an Atlanta Falcons uniform to her left. "The question many are asking today is whether Carl Taylor's condition is Alzheimer's or the result of all those hits he took throughout his career."

"Damn." Nash hit mute when they switched to a story about the upcoming heavyweight boxing match.

"Sorry, man. I thought you should know, so you could prepare."

"Thanks." He heard the toilet flush down the hall and knew his dad was awake. "Listen, Dad's up. I've got to go."

"Let me know what I can do."

"Yep." Trouble was, the kind of help he needed, Ethan couldn't give.

13

Nash rarely gave the Monday-morning quarterbacks much attention. Even so, he put on ESPN News for company as he set his messy house to rights after a busy two weeks on the road for away football games and caring for his dad when he was in town. He was aware from his coaches and staff that the commentators at last week's game were saying he needed to have his head examined after what could have been a suicidal play call on fourth and long with only two minutes left in a game where the Bobcats were down by a touchdown.

Thanks to Shelby's insistence, he'd gone with her odds on fourth down conversions against Savannah State deep in their territory.

It had paid off with a touchdown and a two-point conversion to win the game.

Two popular sports pundits were debating the call. The game had been broadcast on ESPNU, and they had footage of Shelby in the box with the coordinators. ESPN was calling her the Bobcats' secret weapon, which made Nash grin with pride.

After the story, he clicked off the TV and went in search of food, taking his phone into the kitchen with him. Opening up his email, he saw one from Kim, the team's PR person. Nothing unusual there, but when he opened the email, he stopped short. It was about his latest secret weapon. ESPN wanted to do a story on Shelby.

THE FOLLOWING WEEK, Ethan, Sam, and Delaney gathered on the sofa in Nash's living room awaiting the ESPNU segment on Sterling's new statistician.

Nerves had Nash reaching for another beer. He'd been interviewed more times than he could count, going back to his high school days, but today he was nervous for Shelby. A pre-recorded segment with vignettes from this year's football season, along with commentary from him and his coordinators, would be followed by a live interview of Shelby in the small recording studio in the Bobcats' stadium.

He collapsed onto the sofa, and Ethan gave him a slap on the shoulder with a laugh. "Relax, man. She's going to be great."

Delaney chimed in, "She's going to rock this interview," followed by Sam, "Girls rule!"

"Here it is!" Delaney said, picking up the remote and turning up the volume.

Nash sat forward on the edge of the sofa.

A recent headshot of Shelby flashed up on the screen next to the anchor's head as he started off the segment, "The Oakland A's had Paul DePodesta, and now the Sterling Bobcats have Dr. Shelby Wentworth."

"Woohoo!" Delaney clapped her hands. "She looks awesome!"

The anchor recapped the gutsy call Nash and his staff made at last week's game, complete with video of Shelby in the booth, looking adorable in her headset.

"Now we'll head over to Simone, who's got the Bobcats' not-so-secret weapon, Shelby Wentworth."

The scene switched to a beautiful blonde against the familiar backdrop of the Bobcats' studio. "We're here in the Bobcats' stadium with Dr. Shelby Wentworth, number-cruncher extraordinaire."

"Oh my god! Look at her!" Delaney clapped a hand over her mouth. "Sorry," she muttered behind her hand.

Yeah, look at her, Nash thought. She looked amazing. Confident.

"Shelby, let's start with, 'How'd this come to be?'"

She smiled, an easy, relaxed smile. Who knew she'd be such a natural in front of the camera?

"Well, Simone, I've always loved numbers, and I've always loved sports. It just made sense to combine my two loves in an effort to support the Bobcats' bid for the Division I FCS Championship."

"The coaches say you're a genius when it comes to numbers."

A laugh, and then a blush, "I don't know about that, but I will say I love what I'm doing. These are amazing athletes, and the coaching staff are some of the best people I've ever worked with. It's really easy to perform at your best when you're surrounded by the best."

The interview lasted about three minutes, and Nash must have held his breath the entire time. When it ended, he sagged against the back of the couch as Simone wrapped it up. "This may change the future of college football. All teams are going to want their very own Dr. Shelby Wentworth. Back to the ESPN studios."

Delaney brushed an imaginary tear off her cheek. "So proud. Our girl's all grown up."

Nash's chest filled with pride. And something else. Something that felt a whole lot like love.

SHELBY DROVE out to Nash's to meet up with the gang, her head in the clouds. Excitement. Satisfaction. Happiness. All feelings that had long been absent from her life now coursed through her.

The sports world was sitting up and taking notice of her skills. Skills she'd grown to doubt after years with Charlie. Nash had taken a chance on her, and she'd proven her value —to herself, to her team, and to him.

Turning into the driveway, she saw her "tribe" as Delaney called them, waiting on the front porch, all holding signs made out of her headshot like she was some kind of superstar. Tears welled in her eyes. She had a tribe. After years of feeling isolated, and then outright ostracized by Charlie's people, their support meant more to her than they could have ever known.

Brushing back the tears, she laughed and shook her head as she climbed out of the car. When she reached them, Delaney asked, "Can I have your autograph?"

Nash snorted. "You never asked for mine."

She swept her hand at him in dismissal. "Cause I don't want yours. I'm talking about my sister, here." She held out the photo sign and a Sharpie to Shelby. "Just sign it, 'To Delaney, my best friend in the whole world.'"

Nash rolled his eyes then winked at Shelby, and she felt that wink all the way down to her toes. She took the marker and did as Delaney asked.

"Come on." Nash held out his hand. "I've got a glass of champagne with your name on it."

She drew back in surprise.

"Your first interview on national TV—that's something to celebrate." He pulled her close, and leaning in, he murmured, "I'm so proud of you." Her face heated at the intimate contact, especially in front of the tribe, but it was the warmth around her heart that reminded her, once again, of the danger of falling for Nash.

ELATED BUT EXHAUSTED, Shelby said goodnight to her friends. It had been an amazing day, but having good friends to share it with made it one of the best days of her life. And then there was Nash.

"I have to thank you," she said to Nash as he picked up empty beer bottles.

"For what?" He stopped with his hands full and looked at her.

"For giving me the best job I've ever had. I've never felt so excited, so energized, by my academic work."

He set the bottle back down then stepped up behind her and closed the door.

Laughing, she turned to him. "But I was about to leave myself—"

She stopped short when she saw the heat in his eyes. "Stay." He set his hands on her hips, pulling her closer.

"Nash. We've been over this. I work for you. This isn't right." She'd already had a relationship at work that turned out to be the worst thing she'd ever done. She couldn't do it again. Even if it *was* with Nash and her body was singing a different tune.

"Okay, you're fired." He backed her up against the front door and leaned into her. She didn't know which was harder, the door at her back or the man in front of her.

"What about next week's game?"

He pressed kisses along her jaw. "I'll rehire you Monday morning," he said against her neck, sending delicious shivers dancing along her spine.

Giggling as he nuzzled her neck, her amusement quickly turned to lust when he nipped her earlobe. Her resolve began to fade as his hands glided up her ribcage, over her shoulders, then down her arms. That resolve disappeared altogether when he captured her wrists and lifted her arms above her head, pressing his erection into her.

They both moaned at the contact. "Shelby," he whispered, his breath tickling her ear. "Stay."

Then his mouth captured hers, silencing any protests and eliminating any coherent thoughts.

Nash held Shelby's wrists in one hand and slowly opened the silky blouse she'd worn for her interview. She'd looked so beautiful and poised on TV, in a blouse the color of pumpkins in the fields not far from his house.

He'd never seen her in anything silky, and yet, now he couldn't wait to shed her of it. As silky as the blouse felt beneath his touch, he knew the feel of her skin was even silkier.

Her breath caught as he cupped her breast.

He'd kept his hands to himself since the night his father went missing, but he couldn't do it any longer. He wanted her more than any other woman he'd ever known. Consequences be damned.

Releasing her wrists, he slipped the blouse from her shoulders then unzipped the back of her skirt and let it slide to her feet. She stood before him in nothing but flesh-colored bra and panties and a pair of borrowed heels from Delaney.

Desire surged through him, hot and impatient.

Wrapping his hands around her thighs, he lifted her. "Wrap your legs around me."

She whimpered when her core met his.

"Please tell me you're on birth control." He stared into her eyes, their amber depths glowing. She nodded. "You trust me?" his voice rough with barely suppressed desire.

"Yes."

"I want to feel you, Shelby. You, with nothing between us."

He made short work of the buttons at his fly, shoved her panties aside, then plunged into her.

"God, Shelby. I've wanted you like this since . . . forever."

He gazed down at her as her eyes flicked open. He'd never known a more beautiful woman in his life. Stephanie had been beauty-queen perfect. Perfect hair, perfect makeup, perfect nails. But Shelby didn't need any help. She was perfect just the way she was. Especially with the flush of passion on her face.

"You have?" she asked, her eyes wide with wonder.

"Yes." He pressed his lips to her forehead in a tender kiss, and she felt tears burn behind her eyes. It wasn't the three little words, but it was enough. For now.

Taking his face in her hands, she tugged his mouth

down to hers, pouring all of her unspoken emotion into a kiss so searing she expected to see scars tomorrow.

He filled her, inflaming her, as he began to move. Laying her head against the door, she rode the storm.

Holding her tight, he carried her away. Away from the previous year's hell. Away from the new problems this created for both of them. Carried her to the very brink of Heaven.

14

———

They'd managed to make it to Nash's bed for round two. Now, with Shelby's warm body wrapped around his, he couldn't think of another place he'd rather be.

Which was a problem.

He'd originally hired her because he'd wanted to help her. He figured he'd give her a job for the remainder of the football season and she'd earn some extra money to get back on her feet. Instead, not only had he put them both in a precarious situation, she'd also proven herself invaluable to the team, and he didn't want to lose her.

Now he wanted a chance to explore where this could go. And the only way he could do that would be to fire her. Or ask her to quit.

Rock, meet hard place.

He closed his eyes against the pain that caused. Especially after she told him how much she loved the job. And if she quit, how would she be able to pay off her debts?

"I think I smell something burning," Shelby muttered, a

contented smile on her face. "What are you thinking about?"

"I'm pondering the imponderable."

She sat up. "What are we going to do, Nash?"

"I don't know." He sighed, then skimmed a finger along her cheekbone.

What if he gave her a choice—him or the job? What if she picked the job? How could he work with her, see her almost daily, and not have her?

"Truth or dare?" Nash asked, trying to take his mind off the clusterfuck he'd created.

"Truth."

"Who was the first person you had a crush on?" he asked as he stroked her hair.

"You."

He sucked in a breath as his heart performed a slow roll in his chest. Not the answer he'd expected. "Really? How come you never said anything?"

"Because I knew you didn't feel the same." She plucked at the edge of the blanket.

He sat up. "Whatever made you think that?"

She sat up as well. "Seriously? You're asking me that? How about senior prom?"

Nash scrubbed his face. *Oh. That.*

"When you asked Leandra Lucas instead of me? And then had the balls to run off my date on top of it?"

Shit. How had she found out about that?

"Who, by the way," she continued, "didn't bother to let me know he was breaking our date. He just didn't show up. I sat there in my hand-me-down dress for two hours waiting for the doorbell to ring, and it never did."

The icepick to his heart the image conjured left him breathless with regret and pain. He knew Rick "the Dick"

Clemons was a jerk, but he never thought he'd just stand Shelby up. He figured he'd made up some excuse for why he couldn't go.

She got up, began picking her clothes up off the floor, and put on her bra. She thrust her arms into the sleeves of her blouse then realized it was on inside-out. Yanking it off with a growl of frustration, she tried again.

"God, Shelby. I never thought he'd stand you up. I can explain."

"Where have I heard that before?"

"It's not what it seems." He threw the covers back, grabbed his jeans, pulled them on commando and gave them a quick zip.

"And the comebacks just keep getting better and better. Next you'll be saying it's me, not you."

Damn. He was, but only because it was the truth. He had to do something. She searched beneath the covers and came up with her panties then stepped into them. "Shelby, stop." Spinning around, she located her skirt in a heap by the door. Scooping it up, she drew it on, and as she zipped it looked around for her shoes.

"Dammit, Shelby. Stop." He took her by the shoulders and leaned down to make eye contact, but she kept looking away. Taking a chance, he pulled her into his arms. "I never meant to hurt you. You have to believe that."

She relaxed into him, but before he could breathe a sigh of relief, she sniffed. *Ah, man!* She was crying.

He was the world's biggest dick.

"I trusted you," she whispered against his bare chest. "You may not have had the same feelings for me that I had for you, but I trusted you. And you let me down."

He closed his eyes. And now he felt like he'd been kneed in the balls.

SHE PUSHED AWAY from his warm, bare chest and swiped at her tears. She swore that, after all the tears she'd shed over Charlie, she'd never cry over a man again. Let alone over a man who never felt that same for her that she had for him.

"Oh, Shelby." He kissed her hair. "Come here."

He pulled her over to the chest sitting at the foot of the bed and sat her down. Turning to her, he took her hands in his big calloused ones, his thumb caressing the skin there.

"When we were all fourteen, and Ethan and I were in the throes of puberty, we took notice of you as a girl for the first time. We realized we had to take action if we wanted to keep our three-way friendship intact. We made a pact. You were off limits to both of us. That way, there would be no rivalry between Ethan and me. And no awkward decisions for you to make."

"But—"

"We were both in love with you."

"You were?" Was he still, she wondered? Or had it only been a hormone-induced crush?

"Yes. And being the horny little teenagers we were, we both wanted you. Bad."

Definitely a hormone-induced crush. "Didn't I have any say in the matter?"

"No. Not when it came to best friends."

She huffed out a laugh. "Then what changed?"

"By senior year, I had it so bad for you. And after that kiss in Ethan's car, well, I thought maybe you wanted me too. And that couldn't happen. I couldn't break my promise to Ethan."

Shelby remembered that kiss like it was yesterday. No explanations required.

"So you asked Leandra to prom?"

"Yes. And if it makes you feel any better, the date sucked. I think she liked the *idea* of going to prom with me, but she didn't really like *me*. She just wanted to make Cade Newcastle jealous."

"Then why did you scare Rick away? Wasn't it enough that I didn't go with you? You had to completely destroy my senior prom?"

"After I asked Leandra to the prom, I overhead Rick talking with Cade in the boys' locker room. Cade bet Rick he couldn't get you to go to prom with him, and then Rick bet not only would you go to prom with him, but he'd be in your pants before the night was over. I couldn't let that happen."

She stood, her anger back. "Didn't you trust me to stand up for myself? Did you think I would fall for Rick's come-ons? Give me a little credit, Nash."

"You're right. Of course, you're right. It's just . . ." He stood, placed his hands on her shoulders. "I couldn't bear the thought of his hands on you. At all. Not even while you were dancing, let alone . . ." He shook his head.

"If he'd tried anything more than that, I would have kneed him in the nuts."

Nash laughed. "Yeah. You would have." Then his expression turned serious, and he cupped her face in his hands. "I'm so sorry, Shelby. I had the best of intentions—honor my pact with Ethan and protect you from a sleaze ball." He pressed his forehead to hers and closed his eyes. "Can you forgive me?"

Wrapping her hands around his wrists, she sighed. "Yes. Your loyalty is one of the things I love about you."

He pulled her mouth up to his, captured her lower lip in a gentle kiss, then released her. "Come back to bed, and I promise to make it up to you," he said with an irresistibly sexy grin.

And, God help her, she did.

"SHELBY. WAKE UP." He gave her a gentle nudge. "Wake up." She lay curled on her side, the sheet down around her waist, revealing creamy skin and sexy curves.

Damn, he hated to start a day with bad news. He'd much rather start it buried deep inside Shelby.

She groaned then rolled over, throwing her arm over her face, baring her beautiful breasts. He held back a groan of his own, then sat on the edge of the bed.

Sitting up, she pulled the sheet up to cover her chest. Thank God, because he was getting pretty distracted. "What time is it?" She ran her fingers through her hair.

"Seven-ten."

"What is it?" Then she tensed. "It's not your father, is it?"

He handed her one of his T-shirts. "No. But you're going to want to get dressed for this."

Tugging his T-shirt on—lucky T-shirt, he thought—she looked over at him as if waiting for him to drop the bomb.

"Kim Sacks from PR called me this morning. It seems your ex posted some pretty nasty and damning comments on ESPN's website in response to your segment. He's also taken to Facebook and Twitter."

Shelby stiffened and sat bolt upright. "Like what kind of comments?"

"Saying you ruined his career, that you falsified the data and then blamed it on him, reported him to the NIH to get back at him for having an affair."

Her face had gone white, and dammit it killed him to be the one to cause it.

"Don't worry, we'll fight it. Our lawyers will get ESPN to pull down the comments, contact Facebook and Twitter, get them to shut down his accounts."

Shelby looked away then back at him, gnawing on her lip, her eyes wide. Then she just shook her head. "You can't protect me from this," she whispered. "This isn't Tonya Jordan in the schoolyard or Rick trying to get into my pants."

"Shelby, the man is lying. That's defamation. We'll get our lawyers to take care of it." At her continued silence, he got an odd feeling, like when his opponent was about to run a fake field goal play. "He is lying, right?"

"Up to a point."

"Up to what point, exactly?"

SICK TO HER STOMACH, Shelby dragged in a breath. "He is right that I ruined his career, that I reported him. But I didn't falsify the data, and I didn't report him because he cheated on me." She hung her head and muttered, "I didn't find out about that until after."

"Dammit, Shelby. We need to know these things, so we can take evasive action if we need to." He paced away and scrubbed a hand down his face.

"I'm sorry, Nash. First, I didn't think he'd even see the segment, and second, I didn't think even he could sink this low."

Nash stood, hands on his hips. Prompting her, he said, "You reported him."

"Yes." She cleared her throat. She had been the one to

discover that her then-husband had falsified important research data.

"While analyzing data on our last study, I came across something that didn't look right. First, I thought it was an error, so I talked to Charlie about it. His answers didn't add up. Literally. So I looked over the raw data again." She tucked her hair behind her ear.

"Then, before confronting him, I carefully reviewed the raw data on previous papers and found the same issues."

"Why hadn't you seen it before?" Nash asked as he sat on the end of the bed.

"Because he'd been careful—at first—but then he'd become sloppy or cocky, or both. With each paper, the falsification grew bolder."

"In retrospect, I can see his progression. The more articles published with false data without discovery, the more arrogant he became. The more flagrant his data falsification, the more controlling he became, and the more demeaning he became."

"You said he often berated you in front of your colleagues. That he called you stupid. He knew, if anyone could discover his falsification, it would be you. So, he became more and more controlling, undermining both your self-confidence and your stature in the research community."

"Yes. And because over the years he'd made me question my skills, he made me doubt my own work."

It assuaged some of her guilt that, without hindsight, she wouldn't have caught the first few problem papers because the falsification had been so subtle.

"When I finally confronted him about it, he got defensive, then belligerent, then downright hostile and threatening."

"Of course he did. He was a bully. No different than Tonya or any other bully."

Squeezing her eyes shut against the pain, she recalled that fateful encounter.

"Everyone does it," he'd argued. "Don't think for one minute they don't. You think you're so high and mighty. You'd be nowhere without me and my reputation."

"A reputation you built on lies and false data," she'd responded. "All those papers, journal articles, and presentations, with my name on them." She'd felt sick. "And none of them were accurate."

His shame-faced defiant look had said it all.

Her whole career had been built on a lie.

"You report it, and you go down with me," he'd threatened.

"I'd rather have to rebuild my career than go on basing it on lies and false data."

Clenching her fists against the pain of that memory, she continued, "I told him if he didn't report it, I would. He refused, so, I called his bluff and reported it."

She sighed. "After a year-long investigation by Stanford and the National Science Foundation, all our journal articles were retracted, except for the first one, which was my Ph.D. dissertation. Charlie lost his job and was prohibited from receiving federal grant money." She snorted in disgust. "Our so-called friends and colleagues couldn't distance themselves fast enough."

She'd been acquitted, but that didn't matter. Her career, her life, would never be the same again. He may have been a pariah for cheating, but she was a bigger pariah for reporting it.

As if that weren't enough, Charlie had confronted her after he'd received the ruling on his appeal.

"You ruined my career."

"Your career? My career is ruined too," she'd pointed out.

Charlie had stepped into her, his expression nasty. "And whose fault is that? If you'd just kept your mouth shut you'd be—"

"I'd be what, Charlie? The ex-wife of a man who cheated on her instead of the ex-wife of a man who not only cheated on his wife but the whole scientific community?"

Their attorneys had had to step in to break it up.

The humiliation of that confrontation in front of faculty and students had sealed her fate. She couldn't stay at Stanford. It had been time to move on.

She shook her head at the memory. "I had been his doormat for so long."

"Until your integrity was at stake. Then you stood up. Fought back."

"And look where it got me." She threw up her hands. "It ruined my career. Sterling was the only university willing to give me a job after that."

He paused, pulling on his lower lip, clearly thinking. Probably wondering what he'd gotten himself into with her. "I know what it's like to start over, Shelby."

"Yes, but it wasn't your fault."

"And you think this was? On what planet is this your fault?" He leaned forward, adding emphasis to his words.

"I reported him. I gave the feds all the evidence they needed to find he falsified data—for years."

Nash rose from the bed and sat next to her, wrapping an arm around her shoulder.

"I think you're the bravest person I've met."

She shook her head.

"You stood up and did the right thing, knowing the

damage it would cause you. The grief, the heartache. Not many people would have done that, even if it *hadn't* meant sabotaging their own careers."

He pulled her into him, and he felt so good. So solid, supportive, and warm.

"And that's why you didn't come to our ten-year reunion."

"Partly."

Shelby felt a huge weight lift from her shoulders. Atlas shrugging off the world. Even so.

"Maybe it's best if I don't travel with the team this week."

"Oh, hell no. We're not going to let this asshole affect the way we do business." He stood up.

"Nash, the last thing I want is for this story to distract the team."

"All this is documented?"

"Yes. It's in the investigation records. And the *Chronicle of Higher Education* followed the whole humiliating story."

"Get dressed."

"Where are we going?"

"To meet with Kim. You're going to tell her the same story, and we're going to fight back."

15

———

Following a big win against Wofford on the road, and just when Nash thought PR had the story of Shelby's asshat ex under control, he got a text from Ethan:

Turn on the local news.

Flipping on the TV, Nash sank to the sofa when he saw Tonya's face wearing a smug expression. She was being interviewed by Suzanne Davies, a local reporter.

"Sleeping with someone just to get a job. It's disgraceful. Sterling High should remove her Valedictorian title. Oh, and her Most Likely to Succeed superlative. Especially if that's how she succeeds." Tonya looked straight into the camera and smirked.

"You wouldn't know success if it came up and bit you on your fat ass." He clicked the TV off in disgust and threw the remote down. It bounced off the sofa cushion and hit the hardwood floor. The back came off, sending the batteries rolling in all directions. "Son-of-a—"

His phone rang. Looking at the screen, he saw it was Ethan and not some reporter.

"Did you catch it?" he asked without preamble.

"Only the end."

"It appears that Tonya has spotted your car at Shelby's late at night—"

"Talking about stats," Nash defended.

"And that she's seen the two of you holding hands and kissing in public. She went to the media with the story."

"That's bullshit. Shelby and I never kissed in public. Ever the vindictive little bitch." His phone beeped with another call. "It's Shelby, I've got to go."

"Call me later."

Nash switched over. "Shelby—"

"What are we going to do now?" she asked, panic clear in her voice.

"We'll handle it." He paced his living room.

"Handle it how?"

"I don't know. I'll come over so we can discuss it."

"No. People will see your car."

"Then you come here."

"I don't think that's a good idea either."

"Christ, Shelby. No one's going to see your car out here. Why not?"

"Because we have a way of ending up in bed together, and that's what got us into this mess in the first place."

True. "My office then. No one can fault us for meeting there."

"Fine. I'll see you at the stadium in half an hour."

She'd hung up. This was not going to end well. Either she had to give up a job she admittedly loved, costing him one of his best weapons, or he'd have to give her up, costing him his heart.

～

Nash strode down the hall, a set of keys in hand. Shelby stood beside his door looking as if her world had come crashing down. *Dammit.* He unlocked the door to his office and let her in.

The minute they had privacy, she said, "I knew we shouldn't be doing this. And yet, I did it anyway." She threw up her hands. "Seems I can't learn from past mistakes."

"Mistakes?" Nash glared at her. "Is that what we are? A mistake?"

"Of course not, but this is my life, Nash! Not some game. I could lose my professorship over this. Again."

"I know," his tone more conciliatory.

She paced away. "Maybe if I agree to relinquish my position with the football team, they'll let me keep my assistant professor position."

He tossed his keys on his desk. "But you love this job."

"Yes. I do. But I don't have much choice do I? This is the job that prohibits our relationship, not my teaching job. Besides, it's only part-time. It's not like I could live off this job alone." She turned to face him. "It's either that, or we stop seeing each other."

"It's my fault." He released a humorless laugh. "This is what I get for trying to help. I never should have given you the job. I only did it—" He froze. *Holy shit.* What had he just done?

"Only did it for what, Nash?" When he didn't answer, she pushed. "Only gave me the job for what reason?" But the stricken look on her face told him she already suspected.

God, this was not the way he wanted this to come out. He thought a year or two from now, when she had her feet back under her and a successful career as a sports analyst, he'd tell her how it all started.

He sighed. He'd really stepped in it this time. "I hired

you because Delaney saw you looking at the want ad at McGinty's. She guessed, and correctly, that you were having financial problems."

"You—" She stalked toward him, her eyes spitting golden fire. "You hired me out of *pity*? How dare you! How dare you, Nash. I'm not some charity case, someone to take pity on. Why would you do that? Why, Nash?" Her hands fisted at her sides.

"Seemed like a good idea at the time." *What the hell* had *he been thinking?*

"And now I'm paying for it. Again. Just like when I paid for reporting Charlie. No good deed goes unpunished," she muttered. Before he could respond, she continued. "Has this all been about pity? Poor little Shelby? I'll give her a job, take her to my bed. Throw her a bone? Give her a glimmer of hope?"

He reached out for her.

"Don't. Just don't." She crossed her arms over her chest.

Damn, but that hurt, especially when he was only trying to help. "Shelby—"

"No, Nash." She held up her hand, stopping him. "I can't do this."

"Do what? This conversation? The job? Us?"

"None of it, Nash." She turned and walked out.

Hurt, anger, pain, and disappointment collided inside her. Shelby collapsed on her bed, face-down. She'd managed to get out to her car without losing it. She'd even managed to get in her apartment without running into Delaney. But she couldn't hold back anymore. She gave in to the emotions boiling inside her as tears flowed hot and bitter down her cheeks.

She was hurt that Nash felt so much pity for her that he'd hire her on that emotion alone. Did he make love to her for the same reason?

Then she was just as angry at him for giving her a job that she'd fallen in love with. And look where it'd had gotten them both. Her potentially without a job at all, and him with a scandal clouding his winning season.

The pain came from the heart that she didn't think could ever be broken again. How can you break something that is already so shattered, it shouldn't be possible to break anymore?

Finally, she was disappointed in herself. She'd been down this road before, and she'd allowed herself to do it all over again, knowing what the consequences could be.

Even if she could keep her teaching position, how could she face the ridicule of her colleagues and students? It was Stanford all over again.

It would be a toxic work environment, all of her own creation. And with no savings and no prospect for another position, especially now, she'd have nowhere left to go. Who would want her?

Even so, all that paled in comparison when she thought about never seeing Nash again. Never feeling his traitorous arms around her. Never hearing him whisper her name in the middle of the night.

Even after what he'd done, she still loved him. And probably always would.

~

NASH STARED down the neck of his beer and sighed. What a clusterfuck.

McGinty's was quiet on a Tuesday afternoon. Thank God. He was in no mood to talk to anyone, but neither did he want to sit alone in the silence of his house. He knew Hugh would leave him be, so he'd pulled up a seat at the bar and ordered a Scotch ale.

He'd really screwed up this time. He'd screwed up his professional life and his personal life. He'd brought scandal to his team when the focus should have been on their undefeated season.

The athletic director had chewed him a new one, and rightfully so. Feeling like he was more of a distraction than an inspiration, he'd handed off practice to his offensive coordinator and taken off.

Taking another pull on his beer, he thought about the look on Shelby's face when she'd essentially told him good-bye. He was sorry he'd hired her, because if he had to choose between winning football games with her on his staff and having a relationship with her, he'd pick the relationship. But he may have ruined that too, and for the second time.

He glanced up at the television behind the bar and saw Shelby's picture on the screen. "Fuck." He looked around. No one else in the bar seemed to be paying any attention. Small favor. According to the closed captioning on the screen, ESPN had picked up on the story of his relationship with Shelby and was dragging up her past. His photo appeared next, followed by one of a man he assumed was her ex-husband.

As he watched the network that had recently interviewed her for her impressive skill with numbers rake her over the coals, he felt sick.

Shelby couldn't watch anymore. Flicking off the TV, she paced around her tiny still-unfurnished apartment. The extra money she'd been making she'd used to pay off her attorneys and credit cards. At least there was that.

Once again, she was shamed for a work-related relationship, this time in a very public way. They'd dredged up her past, airing all of her dirty laundry.

Her phone buzzed with yet another incoming text. So far she'd gotten numerous texts from Delaney, Sam, Ethan, and Nash, but she'd ignored them all. This one from Nash she couldn't ignore.

Shelby. Text me back and let me know you're okay. Or I'm coming over.

He couldn't come over. The news media had staked out her house, and his presence would only add new titillating video, so she texted him back with *I'm okay*. Nothing more.

Feeling like a prisoner in her apartment, she paced. What a mess she'd made of her life, once again.

She had a part-time job she loved more than her regular job. But a job she'd acquired only out of pity from the man she loved. And now, not only did she have to choose between that job and the man she loved, she might also lose her teaching position with the university. The job that was her bread and butter.

The urge to get away, to escape, if only for a little while, surged through her. Away from the watchful eyes of the media, her colleagues, and her hometown. Away from Nash, where she could think and reevaluate her life.

Thanksgiving was Thursday, and her mother had been asking her to come visit her and her husband in Miami.

Maybe she'd splurge for a ticket and fly down, lick her wounds, and figure out where to go from there.

16

———

Damn, life sucked sometimes. And now was definitely one of those times.

First Shelby, and now this.

Nash stared out his windshield at the cold, steady rain and wished to be just about anywhere but here. After finally making the decision to move his father into a facility with memory care, this would be his first post-move visit.

He'd found an excellent facility in Decatur, east of Atlanta and a two-hour drive from Sterling. While it wasn't the most convenient location for Nash, it was the best-rated facility in the area, and that was more important.

At only fifty-six, Nash's father's condition had progressed significantly in the last few months. His caregivers had been unable to handle him anymore.

Shutting off the engine, he climbed out of the car, his reluctant feet taking him in the direction of the main entrance.

He checked in with the receptionist then walked around to the north wing where the dedicated memory care section was. It boasted additional security to ensure the memory-compromised residents didn't wander off. A staff member buzzed him in, and, taking a deep breath, he knocked on his father's door, unsure who he would find today.

Carl looked up, a frown on his face. *Uh oh.* What now?

On the TV, a local sports anchor was talking about Carl Taylor, a photo from his father's days with the Falcons on the screen. Seemed Nash and his loved ones were top stories this week, and not in a positive way.

His father pointed a finger at the TV. "They're talking about me. Saying I have Alzheimer's or Schizophrenia. That I've lost my marbles."

Nash scuffed his foot on the floor as anger and shame filled him. "Dad—" When Nash looked back at his father, a tear slid down his father's weathered cheek, and the anger and shame turned to pain. Like after taking a helmet to the gut, Nash felt sick.

His father, eyes filled with sadness, held Nash's gaze. "I don't have Alzheimer's or Schizophrenia. And you need to tell them."

"Dad—"

"I want them to know. I want them to understand, do you hear me?"

Nash wanted to argue with his father. He'd wanted to protect his father from the media, but by doing that, he'd only opened his father's condition up to conjecture and rumor, and sometimes the rumors were more painful than the truth. "Yeah, Dad, I hear you."

NASH HAD BEEN LOOKING EVERYWHERE for Shelby. She wasn't answering his calls or his texts. He had to talk to her. To explain to her about the job, and that, yes, he initially hired her because he wanted to help her, but she quickly proved herself vital to the team. And to tell her he and the Athletic Director had come up with a solution. One he hoped she'd like, if she was willing to give up her full-time teaching position.

He'd circled back to Ruby's for a quick bite to find Delaney, Sam, and Ethan sitting in a booth.

"Nash!" Ethan waved him over, and Delaney slid over to make room for him.

"Have you seen Shelby?" Nash asked, wasting no time with greetings.

"I saw her leave this morning with a suitcase," Delaney said. "I'm sure it hasn't been easy this week with all the news." Taking a sip of her iced tea, she eyed him over the rim of her glass.

"Leave?" Knowing how few belongings she had, he could imagine her moving out just that quick. "Did she say where she was going?"

"Miami."

To her mom's? Nash wondered. "For good?"

Delaney shrugged. "Just a visit."

"Doesn't her mom live in Miami now?" Ethan asked.

"Yep," Delaney supplied, popping the 'p' before giving Nash a mysterious smile. "I even have her address."

"You do?"

"Yep." Another popped 'p.' "But it depends on why you're looking for her."

"What do you mean?"

"I mean, are you looking for her for professional reasons or personal reasons?"

"Both."

"Wrong answer, big guy."

Ethan snorted then choked on his tea. Nash cut him a look.

"What do you mean 'wrong answer'?"

"Unless you're looking to apologize to her, I'm not telling you the address."

"Apologize? You're the one who asked me to help."

"I asked you to help her, not ruin her life."

Nash sighed. Delaney was right. Of course he had to apologize about the job. But he also had to convince her that he loved her.

"Look, I just need to talk to her, okay?" Everyone continued to look at him. "What?"

Delaney took her phone out and started tapping on the screen then looked up at Nash, eyes narrowed. "This better not be about the championship tournament and her mad number skills."

The eyes of the group were on him, judging him, waiting for him to speak. "I love her, okay?"

"Well, all right then." Delaney tapped on the screen once more, and Nash's phone buzzed with an incoming text. An address in Coconut Grove.

"It's about damn time," Ethan said.

"What do you mean? What about the pact?"

"What about the pact? Jesus, we were what, fourteen when we made that pact?"

"What pact?" Delaney and Sam asked.

Nash ignored the question, giving Ethan an incredulous look. "You mean to tell me you never gave a damn about that pact?"

"No. I gave a damn about that pact all through high school, but once you and Shelby left, you were adults, big enough to eat hay. And decide for yourselves if there was anything between you." He draped an arm around Sam's shoulders. "Besides, I've got my woman," he said with a big dopey grin.

Delaney was tapping away on her phone again, then his phone buzzed with another incoming text. He looked at the screen.

What are you waiting for?

The doorbell rang, and since her mother was wrist-deep in the turkey's cavity, Shelby answered it.

"Nash!" She couldn't have been more surprised if the President of the United States had been standing there. "What . . . ? How . . . ?"

"Delaney gave me your mom's address."

"Who's at the door, Shelby?" her mother called from the kitchen.

"A friend."

"I didn't know you had friends in Miami." Then her mother came out wiping her hands on a dishtowel. "Nash? Nash Taylor? Well, I'll be." She cut a glance at Shelby. "I hope you can stay for dinner."

"Thank you, Mrs. . ."

"It's Sutton now, but just call me Amy."

"Thank you, Amy."

"But—" Shelby tried to interject.

"Don't be rude, Shelby. Invite Nash in." Her mom headed back toward the kitchen. "Jerome should be home soon. He'll be thrilled to meet you, Nash."

Realizing she couldn't go anywhere, Shelby opened the door wider to let Nash in and closed the door behind him. Then she stood there, arms crossed.

"It's good to see you, Shelby."

No response.

"Why didn't you tell me you were leaving?"

"I didn't realize I had to."

"Is there somewhere we can talk?"

"What if I don't want to talk?"

"Shelby . . ."

"Fine." He followed her across a cool terrazzo floor to the back of the house where room-length sliding glass doors opened into a lush tropical garden complete with a small pool. The mid-century bungalow reminded him of a vacation rental house his parents had taken him to when he was a little boy.

He shoved his hands in his pockets to keep from dragging her into his arms. "Your mom looks good. Happy."

"She is. She finally found a winner in Jerome."

"She certainly deserves it."

Shelby leaned against the back of a teak lounge chair and waited for him to speak.

"Look, I admit, at first I hired you because I wanted to help." At her scowl, he continued, "Jesus, Shelby, you didn't have any furniture. And your bumper was held up with duct tape."

He was met with another arm-cross. She wasn't making this easy. Not that he blamed her.

"But you proved you were worth far more than what I was paying you. I couldn't have won those games without you and your mad number-crunching skills. And not just your skills—your gut instincts. You have a knack for seeing things in the game that none of us can see."

"Is that the only reason you're here? To get me to come

back for the championship tournament? Because if it is, you've forgotten that I can't work for you anymore."

He wanted to reach out, pull her into his arms, but the distance she'd put between them was far more than the physical distance of four feet.

"That's not the reason I'm here." He gazed into her eyes, hoping to catch a glimmer of emotion. Some indication that what he had to say to her would be welcome. And most of all reciprocated. "Shelby, since the day I saw you in the schoolyard, your hair in messy pigtails, a hole in the toe of your canvas tennis shoe, you've had my heart."

Her mouth stretched into a thin line. "I don't want your pity."

He stepped into her then, pinning her against the lounge chair. "Dammit, Shelby. It's never been about pity." He grazed his fingers down her cheek. "It's been about admiration. Respect."

She shook her head, her tear-filled eyes wide.

"And affection."

"Nash—"

"Let me finish. Even that day when Tonya and her mob were ganging up on you, you had a glimmer of courage behind that fear. And watching as you grew—your self-confidence grew too—it was really something." He swiped a tear that fell. "Seeing your insecurity when you returned. Learning the reasons for it. I wanted to give you a kick in the pants, I wanted to see the old Shelby. The one who didn't take crap from the Tonyas or Charlies of the world. Now I'm asking you to come back with me and stand up for something you love. Don't let these people take that away from you."

"I see." She placed her hands on his chest and pushed.

THE HOPE BLOOMING in her chest had shriveled. Nash was asking her to come back and stand up for her job. Which meant only one thing. The game meant more to him than she did.

Even if the university's leadership let her continue to work for Nash, she couldn't do it anymore. She couldn't see him on a daily basis knowing she'd come in second. That he didn't love her. Her heart couldn't take another blow. It already felt so bruised and battered, it was a wonder it kept beating.

"I'm sorry you flew all this way on Thanksgiving. When I go back, it will be for my job in the mathematics department. If they let me keep it."

"Shelby, I'm not talking about the job, although I'd love to see you fight for that too."

"Then what *are* you talking about, Nash?"

"I'm talking about us." He stepped closer. "I'm talking about you and me."

"I don't understand." She braced her hand on the chair behind her because her legs suddenly wobbled.

"Look, if I have to choose between you and the championship, I choose you. But I'm hoping in this case that I can have my cake and eat it too."

Her heart stumbled when she realized what he was saying. "Nash, are you saying you want me *and* the win?"

"I'm saying I want *us* and the win. I want us to win together."

She threw up her hands. "Have you learned nothing from this week's events?"

"I have. And so has Patrick Gibson."

"Patrick? What does the Athletic Director have to do with this?"

"Everything, since if you say yes, he'll be your new boss."

"I—I don't understand."

"Pat has been so impressed by you that he doesn't want to lose you. In fact, he'd like to use your skills to benefit other sports. He wants to create a new position just for you —Director of Sports Analytics. You'll have to extend your number-crunching to other sports like baseball, softball, and lacrosse. You'll manage a new team of analysts and programmers who support athletics' decision-making by organizing, analyzing, and presenting information, and help the Bobcats put the best possible teams on their respective fields and then play their best games on those fields."

Shelby's mouth dropped. Too stunned to speak, she just stared at Nash.

"Of course, you'll have to give up teaching, at least full-time anyway. I'm sure you could teach a course here or there if you really wanted to." Nash's mouth split into a huge grin. "This solves the nepotism problem."

Then her eyes narrowed and he lost his grin. "Is this more pity?"

"No. Do you think Patrick would create a full-time position to manage a new team of employees out of pity?"

"I guess not."

He closed the gap between them and gathered her into his arms, resting his chin on the top of her head.

"You hurt me, Nash."

"I know. Seems like every time I try to protect you, I wind up hurting you."

"Then stop trying to protect me."

"Now that's the Shelby I know. But, I love you, Shelby.

And no matter what you say, that love makes me want to protect you. It always will. Can you live with that?"

Her eyes teared up again. "I suppose I'll have to. Because I can't live without you. I love you too, Nash."

He lifted her chin and brought his mouth down to meet hers in a kiss that touched her soul.

Her mom stepped out onto the patio and beamed at Nash and Shelby. "Looks like we have a lot to be thankful for this year."

~

"WE'RE IN THIS TOGETHER." Shelby clasped Nash's hand in hers. This wouldn't be easy for either one of them, but especially not for Shelby. The primary purpose of this press conference was to face the questions and rumors swirling about Nash's father's health. But questions about his and Shelby's relationship, her job, and the Bobcats' most recent win that would send them to the championship game would come up as well.

After Thanksgiving with Shelby's mom and Jerome, and a couple days of seclusion in a little bed and breakfast in Coconut Grove, he and Shelby flew back to Sterling for this press conference.

He couldn't help but remember another painful press conference three years ago when he had to face off a room of journalists to announce his retirement. That day he'd been alone. But not today. Shelby would stand by his side, facing her demons, as he would face his.

Nash lifted their clasped hands to his mouth, pressing a kissing on the back of her hand. They walked into the room, hand-in-hand, blinking at the flashing cameras.

Nash approached the podium, glanced down at Shelby then cleared his throat.

"Thank you for coming today. I'll get right to it. There have been rumors that my father, Carl Taylor, has Alzheimer's. I'm here today to put those rumors to bed."

With Shelby's warm hand in his, he could handle any question the reporters threw his way. He could handle anything life threw his way. He'd won something better than any championship. He'd won Shelby.

EPILOGUE

T he roar of the fans was deafening. Nash searched the crowd for Shelby. The trophy presentation would begin shortly, and he wanted her there on the quickly assembled stage with him, the rest of his coaches, and his team. She'd been part of the win. But more importantly she'd become part of him.

Bobcats fans were chanting, "F-C-S! F-C-S! F-C-S!"

His phone buzzed. It had been buzzing with incoming texts since the clock ticked down the last second of the game. But there was only one text he wanted right now. One from Shelby. Pulling his phone out of his pocket, he got it.

Soaked from the Gatorade his players had dumped on him, it was a wonder the phone still worked.

I can't get through the crowd.

Dammit. Grabbing one of the many police officers on the field, he gave him a description of Shelby and asked him to find her and escort her back.

His players and coaches hugged, high-fived, fist-bumped, and back-slapped all around him, but he had only one thing on his mind. Shelby.

The announcer came on and said, "Please turn your attention to the stage for the trophy presentation."

The roar grew.

The NCAA President and FCS Committee Chair stepped forward.

"Coach! Coach! It's time!" His QB, Matt Castle, yelled. "Nash!"

Nash spun to see the big burly police officer cutting a path through the crowd standing on the confetti-littered field with Shelby right behind him.

She finally reached him, and he wrapped his arms around her, burying his face in her hair. "Come on." He released her hand and pulled her up the stairs to stand beside him for the presentation.

After a quick speech from the NCAA President, he turned, "Coach Nash Taylor, it's my honor and privilege to present to you the Division I Football Championship Trophy. Congratulations on an extraordinary undefeated season."

Nash took the trophy and held it high to the cheers of the crowd, his players, and his staff. He'd reached the pinnacle of his coaching career, and, as meaningful as that was, it didn't mean as much to him as the woman standing next to him.

"I'd like to thank this incredible group of guys who have become a family, not just a team. I'd like to thank my coaching staff, and their wives and families, for their hard work and dedication toward achieving this goal. It sounds cliché, but that's why they become clichés—because they're true. I couldn't have done it without them. And then there's Dr. Wentworth." He reached for Shelby's hand and pulled her into his side. "Never underestimate the power of a woman, especially one with data." He leaned over and placed a kiss right on her lips and grinned.

Passing the trophy to his quarterback, he answered the network reporter's questions, but all he really wanted was to get Shelby alone.

After what seemed like a lifetime of questions, he saw his chance.

Pulling her through the crowd and down the stairs, he ducked behind the stage while the reporter interviewed his key players and coaching staff.

Gathering her into his arms, he lowered his mouth to hers for a gentle kiss then pulled back and gazed into her eyes.

"You did it, Nash! You won the championship! And with a team only three years old. I'm so proud of you."

"I'm proud of *us*." He kissed her again. "But winning all the championships in the world wouldn't compare to spending the rest of my life with you. You're my greatest win." Pulling the Gatorade-sodden white satin box out of his pocket, he went down on one knee. "Marry me, Shelby."

Tears filled her eyes, and a smile lit her face, then she threw her arms around his neck, knocking them both to the ground. "Yes!"

At the roar of the crowd, they both turned to see their images on the jumbotron. So much for privacy.

Rebecca Heflin is an award-winning author who has dreamed of writing romantic fiction since she was fifteen and her older sister sneaked a copy of Kathleen Woodiwiss' Shanna to her and told her to read it.

Never quite sure what she wanted to be when she grew up, Rebecca didn't attend college until age 30, and earned her bachelor's in literature, before going on to complete her law degree.

Ever the late bloomer, Rebecca finally turned her attention to fulfilling her dream of writing, and published her first novel at age 48. When not passionately pursuing her dream, Rebecca is busy with her day-job at a major state university.

She and her husband are also co-founders of a non-profit organization, which raises money to help cancer patients and their families.

Rebecca's pen name is an abbreviated version of her great-great grandmother's name: Sarah Anne Rebecca Heflin Apple Smith. Whew! And you wonder why she shortened it.

Rebecca writes women's fiction and contemporary romance, and she is a member of Romance Writers of America (RWA), Florida Romance Writers, RWA Contemporary Romance, and Florida Writers Association. Rebecca and her mountain-climbing husband live in central Virginia.

Sign up for Rebecca's newsletter for all the latest news on upcoming releases, appearances, and contests.

www.rebeccaheflin.com
rebecca@rebeccaheflin.com

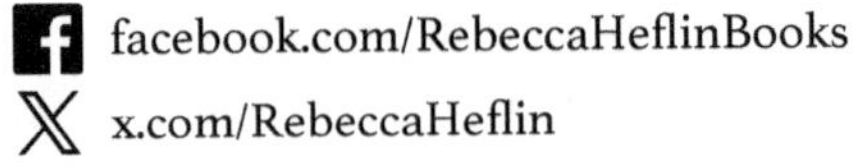

facebook.com/RebeccaHeflinBooks
x.com/RebeccaHeflin

ALSO BY REBECCA HEFLIN

THE PROMISE OF CHANGE

RESCUING LACEY

DREAMS COME TRUE SERIES

DREAMS OF PERFECTION, BOOK 1

SHIP OF DREAMS, BOOK 2

DREAMS OF HER OWN, BOOK 3

STERLING UNIVERSITY SERIES

ROMANCING DR. LOVE, BOOK 1

EDUCATING DR. MAYFIELD, BOOK 3

SEASONS OF NORTHRIDGE SERIES

A SEASON TO DANCE, BOOK 1

A SEASON TO LOVE, BOOK 2

A SEASON TO REMEMBER, BOOK 3

A SEASON TO GIVE, BOOK 4

WHIRLWIND ROMANCE

UNDER THE PARIS MOON